AURELIE

A FAERIE TALE

AURELIE

A FAERIE TALE

HEATHER TOMLINSON

HENRY HOLT AND COMPANY ❦ New York

Henry Holt and Company, LLC
Publishers since 1866
175 Fifth Avenue
New York, New York 10010
www.HenryHoltKids.com

Henry Holt® is a registered trademark of Henry Holt and Company, LLC.
Text copyright © 2008 by Heather Tomlinson
All rights reserved.
Distributed in Canada by H. B. Fenn and Company Ltd.

Library of Congress Cataloging-in-Publication Data
Tomlinson, Heather.
Aurelie : a faerie tale / Heather Tomlinson.—1st ed.
p.   cm.
Summary: Heartsick at losing her two dearest companions, Princess Aurelie finds
comfort in the glorious music of the faeries, but the duties of the court call her,
as do the needs of her friends.
ISBN-13: 978-0-8050-8276-0 / ISBN-10: 0-8050-8276-X
[1. Fairy tales.   2. Fairies—Fiction.   3. Princesses—Fiction.   4. Music—
Fiction.]   I. Title.
PZ8.T536Au 2008   [Fic]—dc22   2007041958

First Edition—2008
Book designed by JRS Design
Printed in the United States of America on acid-free paper. ∞

1   3   5   7   9   10   8   6   4   2

This book is dedicated to Beverly Taylor and Lillian Fedor,
and to the memory of Millicent Schongalla and Louise Stevenson,
lovely grandmothers all.

—H. T.

AURELIE

A FAERIE TALE

CHAPTER 1

Netta

We promised, the three of us. No one would discover that we could see the Fae. Too dangerous, Loic had warned, rubbing his nurse's magic ointment on our left eyes. It stung. I remember blinking through the pain, thrilled at a story come to life: his scaled legs and lizard tail, a boy's arms, torso, and handsome face. After that one solemn moment years ago, the little river drac's hyacinth-blue gaze was never so serious again.

But we believed him. We'd heard Madame Brebisse's tales around the fire of a night, while Princess Aurelie polished her flute and I arranged my mother's needles on a piece of felt. The boy from Skoe, Garin, would even put aside his book to listen. The princess's old nurse said that lesser Fae, lutins and farfadets, were a mixed lot. If a farmwife left honey cakes on her back step, they might repay her by caring for sick animals and fixing broken tools. Or they might tease her rooster into crowing all night. Other Fae, like the skeletal White Ladies, dragonlike gargouille, and shape-shifting river drac, preyed on men. *Their* attention could be fatal.

Summer after summer, we kept our friend's gift a secret, meeting by the river to play Seek the Princess and Skoeran Pirates. Later, Loic would transform himself into different shapes to amuse us. It was all glorious fun, until one market day in Cantrez, the year I turned fifteen. As I left the bakery with a hot braided loaf for Aurelie, I saw a suck-breath stalking a baby.

It looked like a bundle of sticks wrapped in wrinkled gray skin and topped with a shock of white hair. The suck-breath, not the baby, who slept in a basket under Rosine the flower seller's table.

A night nuisance, suck-breaths. I'd never seen one abroad in daylight before, and perhaps that's what rattled me. Like a fool, I walked straight over to it. Rosine was busy helping the butcher's wife select roses and greenery for her daughter's wedding party. I crouched to coo at the baby. The suck-breath hissed and twitched away from the bread's yeasty scent. I broke a piece off the braided loaf, took a bite, and chewed, my throat dry. The rest I dropped into the basket.

Casually, I thought, but Rosine noticed. Suck-breaths were invisible, but in Cantrez, mothers knew what the bread meant. Or else she had smelled the odor of vinegar and old shoes that clung to the ugly Fae. It was nothing like Loic's scent of river reeds and moist earth and musk.

"Good morning, Netta." The flower vendor greeted me, then bent to smooth her baby's blanket. When she stood up, she set the basket on the table beside her, out of the Fae's reach. The baby gurgled and was quiet again. "How fares the royal household this fine day?"

"Well, thank you, Rosine," I answered. We chatted about the weather and the dress my mother had made for Princess Aurelie (raspberry silk, trimmed with creamy white ribbons and lace I'd made myself, a new pattern from the capital) and whether Queen Basia's delicate health was improving in the mountain air.

Denied the baby's milky breath, the disappointed suck-breath kicked over two tall pails of sunflowers and another of irises, and stamped away.

"Ah, clumsy!" Rosine said to no one in particular. "Give me a hand, would you, Netta?"

"Of course." I picked up a pail and fetched more water from the fountain. Gathering the fallen stems, we quickly set the stall to rights. When we'd finished, Rosine gave me a bouquet of irises. She wouldn't accept payment.

"No, thank *you*, Netta." She stroked her baby's head, and we both knew what she meant. I hoped she wouldn't tell anyone what had—or hadn't—happened.

The irises were the color of Loic's eyes, a deep, rich blue, almost violet. Mountain-born folk, like the queen's family and my own, had dark eyes, brown or black. The foster boy Garin's were a changeable gray-green, and King Raimond's a steely blue. But looking into Loic's eyes was like watching a piece of the night sky just before the stars came out. It made me feel the same way, hushed inside but joyful, too. Like listening to Aurelie and her mother play their flutes or swimming in the river on a summer morning, water sliding cool along my skin.

As I retraced my steps to the bakery for a new loaf, I spotted the rare, magical color again. This time it was on the coat of a gentleman in plumed hat and buckled shoes who was inspecting the pistols displayed in a gunsmith's window.

At least, that's what my right eye told me. My left insisted on a lizard's tail under the coat, the sheen of scales, and a wispy blue fin that sprouted from the drac's back to drift in an unseen current. Watching him with both eyes made me dizzy, as if the two shapes, Fae and human, didn't belong in the same space. Though smaller, Loic shimmered like that whenever our games took him far from the river.

I realized that I was gawking at the father of my secret friend. Fear fluttered in my throat; my cheeks burned. I stared at my shoes and hoped he wouldn't notice me. Prayed the suck-breath hadn't tattled. It was too late to turn around; the bakery was on the other side of the gunsmith. If I'd been clever, like Garin, or brave, like the princess, it might have been all right. But I wasn't.

"Good day, mademoiselle," he said. "What lovely flowers."

His voice made me think of vanilla custard sliding off a golden spoon. Madame Brebisse said the drac used that voice to lure his victims into the river. People who amused him and his wife would be released after a night of feasting in their underground palace. Dull guests paid for the privilege with their purse. I'd never asked Loic what happened to those both poor and stupid, but I assumed I was about to find out. Aurelie would have given the drac a polite smile and forged on; Garin would have eased away with a witty remark. I wasn't as strong.

As lazily as a toad catches a fly, the drac's voice snagged the disastrous truth from my lips. "You're kind to say so, monsieur le drac," I stammered.

Immediately, I wished I had bitten my tongue. Idiot! I knew better than to acknowledge one of the Fae when he wore a human shape. I curtsied, hoping the drac would overlook the slip and let me pass.

Instead he seized my elbow and twisted, jerking me upright. "I beg your pardon, mademoiselle?"

"That is," I flailed, as if we were still discussing flowers. "The irises are much prettier growing wild along the river, aren't they? A bolder blue, and yellow—" Even to my own ears, my voice sounded guilty.

"You recognize me?" Each word hard as diamond.

"No," I said, my face hot. "I'm sure we've never been introduced, monsieur."

The drac's voice was almost gentle. "Alas, mademoiselle. It grieves me, but I cannot permit a mortal, even one as charming as yourself, such familiarity with my affairs."

"P-please, monsieur," I stuttered.

"How did you come by your so-acute perception, I wonder?" the drac inquired.

At least I could protect my friends. I locked my chattering teeth on the answer and stared hard at the irises. I'm not sorry; their celestial blue flags were the last thing I saw before the drac's claws stabbed out and blinded me.

CHAPTER 2

Aurelie

"What is hidden, shall be revealed." Exultant, the woman's low voice wound around the notes.

As if revealing things was a *good* idea. Standing behind a screen in the cathedral, Aurelie clutched her flute, hands sweating on the polished wood. She decided that the requiem's composer had never met the Fae, or paid the price for betraying their secrets.

The singer hadn't either. She sang as if she offered a precious gift to the cathedral full of mourners. The choir's massed voices joined in. "And nothing remain unavenged."

Another lie. What about Netta? Who had avenged Aurelie's poor, blind friend?

Nobody. Because nobody knew the truth about what had happened two years ago, except Netta herself and Garin and Aurelie. They hadn't even told Loic, before the war began and everything changed.

The next time Aurelie had visited Cantrez she'd found the Fae's river-bank home abandoned. Dracs didn't fear human vengeance, so they must have had their own reasons for leaving it.

Though sung with conviction, such words were empty promises. And yet the beauty of the music pulled Aurelie's attention upward, along tall stone columns to an enormous many-petaled window set under the vaulted roof. Slivers of red glass pulsed against the pale stone like embers blazing in a bed of ashes. The colors swam before Aurelie's eyes. She blinked, bracing her shoes against the stone floor. She wouldn't faint at the service commemorating the first anniversary of her mother's death. At least not before it was her turn to play.

Yearning, the melody climbed. The men's deep voices fell away, and then the women's, as if the music traveled to a place where only the most innocent could go. Aurelie walked out to stand by the choir. As reverently as she could, to honor the mother who had taught her how to play, she lifted her flute and joined in.

One voice accompanied her, a child's clear treble. "Eternal light shine on them."

Aurelie's neck prickled with heat; her face felt flushed under the strip of veil. She couldn't have prevented the fever that killed her mother, but if she had acted differently two years earlier, if she hadn't sent her friend to the market square where she met the river drac, or had accompanied her, at least…how different life might be. For Netta, most of all, but for Aurelie, too, and poor little Loic. How abandoned he must have felt when his mortal friends stopped visiting so abruptly.

She couldn't let tears choke her breath. Not here, not now. Aurelie emptied her mind and played. When her part ended, she lowered her flute and bowed her head, the knot of red-brown hair heavy against her collar. That was the only movement in a crowd that filled the wooden benches to overflowing. Lumielle's townsfolk and merchants, courtiers and farmers, artisans and servants alike seemed transfixed. Not one stirred, holding tight to the delicate thread of sound.

"Because thou art merciful." Alone, the child's voice soared toward the heavens.

Aurelie wished she could believe in truth being revealed and errors forgiven. But she had seen injustice at close quarters, enough to strip her of childish illusions. Ten years, not two, might have separated her from the girl who had played with a drac child. As Heir, the responsibility for a kingdom rested squarely on Aurelie's shoulders, reminding her to measure every word. And yet, while she listened to that angelic voice, she could imagine freedom. If only her mind could lift from her body, from her roiling stomach and the sweat that slicked her skin. The pure notes hung in the air, beckoning. She reached for the comfort the music offered; she almost had it....

The child's voice faded. The rest of the choir returned with a roar, finishing in a ringing chorus. The cleric stood to bless them. The service had ended.

Aurelie smoothed disappointment into a gracious court mask. She still had to get out of the cathedral gracefully. And to the gravesite, and through her afternoon's appearances, and onto the ship. If she told her father of the fears that troubled her, the diplomatic mission to Dorisen would be delayed again, which her country could ill afford. She had to go and hope for a calm sea crossing to the Skoeran capital.

If the weather didn't oblige, at least she'd have vomited herself clean of all emotion but the desire to touch dry land again.

With a soundless sigh, Aurelie took her place in the procession down the aisle. When she passed Elise, she handed her flute to the maid and accepted a silk shawl in return. Count Sicard, her father's chief counselor, whispered to her, "How dear Queen Basia would have enjoyed hearing you play. Magnificent, Your Highness."

Aurelie nodded her thanks. A shaft of pain lanced through her chest, stealing her voice. She wanted to run, and keep running. Out of the cathedral, out of the city, and into the mountains, where people called her "cousin," not "Highness." Into the past, where her mother still laughed and sang, where Aurelie played in the woods with her friends, where a boy treated her as his best friend, not the Heir. Where delight, not duty, ruled her life.

It cost her, to maintain the Heir's correct two paces behind her father, down the long aisle and through the press of sorrowful, sympathetic faces. Pushing past clouds of incense, Aurelie reached the doorway at last. King Raimond started down the wide steps, but Aurelie paused to wrap her shawl around her shoulders.

A hush had settled over Lumielle, as if the cathedral's great carved doors had opened onto dawn rather than midday. Dividing the city like a knife cuts a pie, the River Sicaun flowed to the sea in a gray-green ribbon fringed with trees. The capital's usually busy bridges and streets, spiraling outward from the two islands at its heart, were deserted. In the distance, golden stubble shone in harvested fields. Touches of crimson and rust splashed the trees at the festival grounds outside Lumielle's walls. Although too far away to see them, Aurelie fancied that the forest lutins painting their autumnal colors had set down their brushes for a moment, like respectful workmen, to honor the queen's memory. Or perhaps the Fae were avoiding the sound of the bells that tolled from the cathedral tower, deafeningly loud. The vibration thrummed through Aurelie's body as she sucked in deep breaths of cool air, trying to refresh her weary brain.

Soldiers dressed in blue and gold lined the steps down to a broad paved area in front of the cathedral. More of them stood along the wide boulevard and fortified bridge that connected the cathedral's Ile-Dieu to the palace's Ile-Fort. Vaguely, Aurelie noticed how dashing the honor guard looked, their coats decorated with gilt braid and the royal white eagle insignia. There had been little cause for gaiety while Jocondagne's two-year-old disagreement with the island nation of Skoe worsened from hard words and trade blockades to actual skirmishes. When neighboring Alsinha threatened to enter the conflict as well, Jocondagne's nobility had deserted the capital for the relative safety of country estates. Parades and balls, their usual diversions, had fallen out of favor.

With a truce in place and a treaty waiting to be drafted in Skoe's capital, these soldiers must have been glad to pull their parade uniforms out of cedar chests and dusty wardrobes. Of course, Skoeran or Alsinhalese spies might still lurk behind one of the windows overlooking the cathedral. Showing weakness of any kind would hurt her side's position in the upcoming negotiations. Aurelie needed to be strong or, failing that, to appear strong. She tried for a resolute expression.

The soft cough at Aurelie's shoulder startled her. She might have pitched forward, down the wide stairs, if the cleric hadn't grasped her elbow. "Your pardon, Princess Aurelie."

"Yes?" she said.

"The people are waiting for you to precede them."

"Of course." Aurelie's face flamed. How long had she been blocking the way? She picked up her heavy skirts and hurried after her father. When she rounded the side of the cathedral, he was waiting, a wreath of purple flowers in his hand. Silver glinted in the king's light hair. Slate-blue eyes studied her from under the sandy brows. He frowned. "You look unwell, Aurelie. This trip to Dorisen—"

"I'm fine, Papa." She brushed away his concern and nodded at the flowers. "May I?"

"As you wish."

Aurelie took the wreath and stepped into the woodland that covered the southern tip of the Ile-Dieu. As always, the park's ancient trees welcomed her. Feathery branches of evergreens muffled the clamor of the bells; gnarled oak and majestic chestnuts invited her to press her face to their bark and share their deep-rooted strength. Abandoning the path, Aurelie wove between the trees, stripping off her gloves to stroke the sturdy trunks. The wreath's petals tickled her skin. As lightly, a forest lutine reached twiggy fingers out of a copper beech to touch the princess's hair. Aurelie pretended not to notice. After the drac had blinded Netta, ignoring the Fae had become second nature.

To Aurelie, at least. She didn't know about Garin, who'd left Jocondagne shortly afterward with the rest of the Skoerans. Once, that would have been the first of a thousand questions she'd stored up to ask him after the hostilities had eased. Now she wasn't as sure that they could ever recapture their old closeness. Since her mother's death the previous year, Aurelie felt as though her heart had been removed from her body, and, like in one of Madame Brebisse's tales, hidden in an egg, inside a pigeon, in an iron box banded with chains and cast to the bottom of the sea, so deep she could never recover it.

And maybe she didn't even wish to. It was easier to forget one's heart and go along under duty's lash, like her father. After his wife's death, King Raimond had withdrawn into himself, emerging only to conduct the Skoeran war with a sternness unlike his previous patient good humor. It was as if he welcomed having an enemy to distract him from grief. He didn't seem to understand how Aurelie felt as those she cared for had been taken from her, one after the other.

Driven by her unhappy thoughts, Aurelie found herself at the stone slab. She set the wreath above the words carved into the granite top. "Basia of Jocondagne, beloved wife, mother, and queen." The dates followed, and then two mismatched beasts.

The sea eagle made sense. At the center of the royal family's crest, the symbol of House Pygargue spread its broad wings in a gesture of protection. White eagles could be found throughout the palace. Their image ornamented everything from leather book bindings and chair backs to banners, linens, and maidservants' aprons.

"But a *goat*?" Aurelie said aloud.

Her father had come up behind her. "I thought she would like it," he said softly. "Your mother never tried to hide her birth."

Again, Aurelie remembered those long-ago summers at Grand-mère's farm, where Queen Basia had delighted in setting aside the court's protocol and had taught her daughter to make flower garlands and milk Boss Nanny. After a day spent running wild in the woods with her friends, Aurelie would come home and curl against her mother's side, listening sleepily as Madame Brebisse entertained the household with stories of the Fae. Or Aurelie and her mother would play together, two wooden flutes trading one melody between them.

An ache spread through her body. She wished she hadn't left her flute with Elise.

In a rare caress, her father rested his hand on Aurelie's shoulder. "A year already, and it hurts as much as ever. Doesn't seem fair, does it?"

"No." With a sense of relief, Aurelie turned her face into his coat and let out the anguish clawing at her throat.

Nothing was fair! How could it be, when her dearest friend walked in darkness and her mother slept in the ground? Then the stupid war had divided her from the only boy who'd ever seen her, not her crown.

"I know," her father said. "Courage, my dear. A princess thinks first of her people."

"Yes, Papa." Aurelie was tempted to confide in him. But little girls grew into young women with private lives of their own. As another girl might hide her flirtations, Aurelie kept her fears close. If her father knew how she worried about failing in her diplomatic mission to Dorisen, he might go in her place. Or send someone whose loyalties weren't compromised by friendship with a Skoeran. Or worst of all, explain that Aurelie was only a figurehead, that Count Sicard would complete the actual negotiations. The Heir's job was to smile at the other dignitaries and sign where they told her. Unless she offended one of the Skoeran council members, Aurelie wasn't likely to affect the outcome of the talks. Her heart might be missing, but she still had her pride. Aurelie decided she'd rather act as though she had power and be mistaken than know for certain that nothing she did mattered.

But before she left Lumielle for Dorisen, she had to preside over afternoon galettes and hot chocolate at Saint Somasca's Home for Orphaned Children. And attend the banquet for the hospital nurses, giving a short speech to thank them for devotion to their patients. Then, before the evening tide, she must step onto the deck of the ship that would carry her to the capital of the Skoeran isles.

Garin's country. Deep down, under grief and worry, hope burned like a banked coal. Of her three closest friends, Netta refused to come to Lumielle, and Aurelie had no idea where Loic might be. If anyone knew how to make her feel herself again, Garin would. Working together, couldn't they achieve peace?

Aurelie knelt next to her father and touched the grave marker. She traced the goat's head and wiped her eyes dry with the shawl. Then she stood tall, and lied. "I'm ready, Papa."

"That's my brave girl."

If she hadn't looked over her left shoulder, Aurelie wouldn't have seen the Fée Verte glide out from behind a tree and sweep her green mantle over the grave, spangling the ground nearby with the tiny white blossoms that mountain folk called Fairy's Tears.

The rest of that day, Lumielle's residents marveled at the unexpected fragrance wafting through their streets like the last gift of summer. Though she hadn't acknowledged the Fae, Aurelie, too, breathed the scent hungrily until the salt breeze filled her ship's sails and pushed her far from Jocondagne's shore.

CHAPTER 3

Aurelie

Five days later, installed in a guesthouse in Skoe's capital city, Aurelie contemplated the mirror. The setting sun filled the room with golden light and illuminated her reflection all too clearly. "This is your best work?"

The question set her maid and the two local dressmakers to twittering. "Perhaps Princess Aurelie would prefer the jeweled net, à la Leyoness?"

"Oh, no—jeweled net would clash with this soft gray silk. We'd better keep the pearls."

"The present effect is quite handsome. Your Highness will set a new fashion for simplicity, refinement, and—"

Aurelie gestured them to silence. After a full night and day ashore in Dorisen, her fever had dropped and the world had stopped swaying, but pain still throbbed behind her temples. Her stomach felt queasy again; she'd never keep down her food. Not that she expected to eat much. If the inn's menu represented the islanders' general liking for mouth-burning spices, she'd be lucky to find one dish she could sample without weeping tears of pain.

Captain Inglis, the chief of Skoe's governing council, had invited the Jocondagnan representatives to her home for an informal supper. In moments, Aurelie was supposed to meet Count Sicard in the courtyard, and she looked hideous.

Well. Not hideous, exactly. That was unfair to the efforts of the hovering servants, none of whom would meet her eyes in the mirror. Her maid Elise was especially shy around the two local women hired to assist with the refurbishment of Aurelie's wardrobe, which had suffered since Skoeran ships had stopped supplying Lumielle with fine fabrics and other luxuries.

She owed the ghostly pallor of her face to seasickness. A storm had delayed their arrival and kept her shut inside a tiny cabin with an equally ill Elise. Her maid had tried to hide the traces of illness by scrubbing Aurelie's skin, then slathering it with rice powder. Aurelie couldn't find fault with her hair and gown; both had been neatly arranged. After rejecting half a dozen styles as too gaudy, she hardly dared complain when they combed her hair back and laced her into a severe gray gown, although one of her frilly nightgowns could better pass for evening dress than this plain thing! At least the pearl coronet added a touch of elegance.

Aurelie sighed. After studying documents all afternoon, her tired eyes burned. In truth, she looked like the figure on a tomb in the royal chapel. All she needed to complete the resemblance was a stone dog at her feet. Or the big gray cat curled on the window seat. Having withstood Elise's attempts to chase him from the bedchamber earlier, the sleeping animal gave every impression of being carved in stone. Aurelie wished she could borrow his assurance, if only for the evening. "Leave me," she told the servants.

Elise lingered, frowning at the cat and adjusting a ribbon that didn't need fixing. "Don't worry, Your Highness," she whispered. "Ill and all, it's grown-up you look. And tidy. Skoerans are the very demon for neatness. Ship-shape, they say; you'll impress him for certain."

Dabbing orange water on her wrists, Aurelie stiffened. Was Elise insinuating that Aurelie favored one Skoeran in particular? The maid didn't know Garin; he'd left Jocondagne when he was fifteen years old, before Elise had started work at the palace. And Aurelie hadn't spoken of him to anyone in her party, although the ties of trade, a common language and customs meant that many Jocondagnans and Skoerans were acquainted. She breathed shallowly, hoping that would clear her vision. It helped, a little. "Who do you mean?"

"Why, Captain Inglis's son. Hui, his name is. Ever so handsome, the cook told me this morning, and a First of his own ship, though he's not five and twenty."

Her secret was safe. Aurelie's lips curved in amusement that she'd rather be accused of dressing to please a man she'd never met than one who'd once been closer than a brother. And with a maid for a matchmaker, who needed diplomats? Elise sounded quite prepared to secure the peace by marrying off her employer to a Skoeran ship's officer. Aurelie understood enough about statecraft to realize there was more than one reason she'd been included with Count Sicard in this select mission of two. She didn't like being a pawn in court politics, but that wasn't Elise's fault. Or maybe her maid had imagined a star-crossed love between warring kingdoms, that staple of theatrical romances. Skoerans didn't have kings and nobles. Captain was their highest rank, and making First was no small accomplishment.

Aurelie got up and steadied herself against the doorframe, taking slow, careful steps in her new shoes. Gray, to match the dress, with jet buckles. They pinched. "I'm here on diplomatic business, Elise. Not to flirt."

"Yes, Your Highness." The maid curtsied, but the expression on her freckled face said "Why not both?" as plain as speech.

And maybe flirting was a kind of diplomacy, Aurelie thought as she settled onto the bench of one of the odd conveyances, like a tall box with poles fixed to either side, which substituted for carriages in Dorisen. As instructed, she rapped the roof. Two porters, one behind and one in front, picked up the poles and carried her from the guest-house courtyard.

She peered out the window slot, wishing Netta had accompanied her, though they wouldn't have both fit in this box-chair. According to the letters her friend's mother sent from Cantrez, Netta was well. *Bored*, Aurelie thought, reading between the conventional lines. How Netta would have enjoyed the smells, sounds, and tastes of this foreign city! Dorisen's narrow stone step-ways couldn't be more different from Lumielle's tree-lined boulevards and riverside promenades.

From a distance, the chain of islands that made up Skoe resembled a handful of rough stones cast in a child's game. As her ship approached them, Aurelie had seen that the steep hillsides couldn't be cultivated like Jocondagne's fertile river valleys. Skoerans farmed on terraces cut into the hills, and they built their cities the same way, layer upon layer. Since their real wealth came from the sea, from fishing and trade, the Skoeran capital wasn't located on the largest island, but the one with the most protected anchorage. It nestled inside the hollow crater of a long-dead volcano. After the mountain's fire had died, the sea had breached the island's steep sides in two places, creating inlets into an otherwise perfectly round harbor that kept Skoe's merchant fleet safe through the wildest winter gales. Inside the bowl, water lapped quietly at the docks; outside, the ocean beat against the island's rocky shell, creating a low, angry rumble that had disturbed Aurelie's sleep.

As she traveled upward, Aurelie found the sound less ominous. Listening to its rough music, she studied Dorisen's vertical layout with interest. All-important commerce dominated the first and widest terrace at sea level, with wooden docks and stone warehouses, inns, banks, ships' agents, and chandleries. Schools, hospitals, theaters, and other municipal buildings occupied the city's next tier. Like cliff-swallows' nests, residences had been carved into the heights above the rest. Flights of steps connected buildings to one another, and to the roads that spiraled from level to level, crowded with slow-moving ox-carts. The shadows lengthened as they climbed. Aurelie was surprised not to see a single horse. Most people, it appeared, walked to their destinations. The elderly, infirm, and visitors hired box-chairs.

"No shame for you to be carried along the step-ways, Your Highness," one of the Skoeran dressmakers had assured her. "We make allowances for foreigners."

She hadn't said "weak foreigners," but Aurelie had heard the politely omitted word. After spending just a day among the Skoerans, she thought they must be the fittest people she had ever met.

Descending from the chair into a torch-lit courtyard confirmed Aurelie's opinion. She was by far the youngest person to arrive in a box-chair. Most of the captain's dinner guests strolled up to the stone gates on their own two feet, chatting easily, as if a dozen flights of steps shouldn't cause a person to pant for breath. Aurelie also noticed that the mode for tight-fitting trousers on men and shorter skirts on women showed off their elegant calves. Fashionable Skoerans might consider Aurelie's gray gown dowdy, but it did cover her skinny ankles.

And her pearls were fine, the equal of any of the Skoerans' jewels. At least she thought so until Count Sicard led her into the entry hall. They joined the queue of guests surrendering their invitations to the servant who would announce them.

Too mannerly to whistle out loud, the count hissed between his teeth.

Aurelie fingered her invitation. Had they misread? Captain Inglis's "informal supper" had the air of a fancy-dress ball. Her guests were resplendent in gilded brocade and silver tissue, metallic lace and vibrant silks. The men glittered as opulently as the women, their costumes a blend of styles and materials that Skoeran ships must have brought from the far corners of the world. To Aurelie's dazzled eyes, the other guests looked like they'd been rummaging in chests of pirate treasure. What else could have supplied the swags of golden chains ornamented with coins and charms, the ropes of diamonds and pearls, jeweled earrings, necklaces, bracelets, and rings?

The tall Skoeran seamstress had said Aurelie would set a fashion for "simplicity and refinement." Had she intended mockery or warning? So recently enemies, it was difficult to know what emotions lay under the Skoerans' courteous veneer. But Aurelie knew she wasn't imagining the amused, almost pitying looks people were giving her now. She glanced down in chagrin at the severe gray gown.

"Eyes up, Your Highness." Count Sicard squeezed Aurelie's arm, his bluff heartiness unaffected. One of her father's most trusted advisers, the count usually resembled a gentleman farmer, his coat rumpled and hat askew. Tonight he was impeccably dressed in midnight blue. A large sapphire twinkled on his left hand. "Skoerans value wealth that is portable," he whispered. "They flaunt it on formal occasions. By misleading us as to the nature of this gathering, Captain Inglis evidently means for us to be discomfited and begin tomorrow's working sessions at a disadvantage."

Aurelie straightened her shoulders, trying not to mind that only the servants were dressed as drably as she and her escort. "Then we won't give her the satisfaction."

Count Sicard's dry chuckle rewarded her. "Indeed we won't."

They arrived at a blue-draped doorway and tendered their invitations. Like the door curtains, the room's ceilings, walls, tables, and chairs were swathed in aquamarine satin. Hundreds of candles twinkling from mother-of-pearl sconces on the billowing blue made Aurelie feel as if the walls were undulating before her like waves. Mats of woven sea grass perfumed the air, and tapestries pictured mermaids in coral palaces, combing their hair or riding dolphin-back through tranquil oceans. She pushed down the knot of unease in her stomach and aimed her gaze high as she waited to be announced. Netta would be interested in every detail of the colorful scene; Aurelie mustn't let shyness prevent her from observing it all.

The chamberlain thumped his staff on the floor. "Count Sicard, the Jocondagnan emissary, and Her Royal Highness Princess Aurelie of the House Pygargue, Jocondagne's Heir!"

CHAPTER 4

Aurelie

"Welcome, Your Highness." Their hostess crossed the room with a rolling gait, as if she traversed a ship's deck rather than the salon's parquetry floor.

Captain Inglis wore a crimson gown trimmed with knots of gold ribbon and clusters of cherry-sized rubies. Ruby clips held her pale hair away from a weathered face. Light eyes swept over Aurelie from coronet to shoe buckle, as if calculating what price the princess's modest ensemble might bring on the Skoeran market. The rapid inventory completed, the woman bowed first to Aurelie, then to her escort. Her gaze lingered on his jeweled ring. "And Count Sicard. *Enchantée.*" Booming, her voice: pitched to carry over the roar of the waves, rather than the clink of silver and china.

Aurelie curtsied, trying to ignore her pounding head. The woman didn't look like a Skoeran. She was much blonder than the other people present, whose hair tended to nut shades, filbert and walnut. Had she come to Dorisen from Alsinha, or even Jocondagne's north-eastern forests? It wasn't important, really, but odd. "Pleased to make your acquaintance, Captain Inglis."

"Met before, haven't we?" the woman snapped.

Had they? Aurelie bit her lip. Was she supposed to remember the dignitaries she'd been presented to as a child? It had been two years at least since a Skoeran had visited Lumielle's court.

All amiability, Count Sicard bowed. "At a reception several years ago, I believe. We're so pleased to be visiting your beautiful city, and thank you for your hospitality."

"Sail on, sail on," Captain Inglis said. "Come meet the rest of our little party."

Islanders were given to understatement, Aurelie decided. The captain's "little party" at her "informal supper" numbered over fifty superbly dressed guests. Aurelie quickly lost hope of retaining a fraction of their names or titles, since none were Garin Deschutes.

Strangely, there seemed to be no assigned places for the meal. Sitting at a small table with an older couple intent on demolishing a halibut, Aurelie poked at her squid and drained a third goblet of water. She wished the chef had been less generous with the spices. The fiery sauces couldn't disguise the fact that the wide array of dishes, presented in expensive tureens and platters, contained fish, fish, and more fish.

If Aurelie were Skoeran, she'd have been ready to make peace with Jocondagne long since, just for the basket of fresh fruits and veg-etables a handful of coppers would buy in the Cantrez market. The thought of mountain strawberries made her mouth water, although they were a spring taste. In the fall came purple grapes and wedges of sharp cheese, sizzling bacon and galettes off the griddle, slathered with apple butter and dusted with powdered sugar.

"Glad to see you enjoying the devil squid, Your Highness." A bold voice interrupted her reverie. "Most outlanders don't appreciate such delicacies."

"Mm," Aurelie said, as a good-looking young man dropped into the empty seat beside her. Another pair of light eyes, bright as glass chips, regarded her from a tanned face. Dark-haired, tall, he wore a black coat with dull gold piping and plain black trousers.

Aurelie relaxed into her seat. At least one other person hadn't dressed like a buccaneer's pet parrot. She could forgive the gold studs glinting in his ears, it was so restful to look at him. "You thought the party was informal, too?" She gestured from her gown to his equally plain coat.

"What?" He sounded surprised, then laughed. "No, these are ship's dress blacks. Considered suitable for the most formal event."

"Oh," Aurelie said. "Your pardon."

"Don't mention it." With relish, her seatmate cracked open a spiny crustacean. "*Informal* means the serving style," he explained. "The latest rage. Dishes set out on the tables, you pick what you like, sit where you please, then circulate between courses. Not like a banquet, where you're stuck in one chair all night."

"Ah." She studied her lap.

White teeth flashed as he dismembered another sea creature and sucked out the meat. "Claw?" he offered.

She repressed a shudder. "No, thank you."

Without asking, he took some of her squid, chewed, and swallowed. "Delicious. Last bite for you?"

Aurelie opened her mouth to refuse. The stranger tipped the squid into it. "Down the hatch," he said cheerfully, and wiped his greasy hands on a napkin. He didn't appear to notice how the sauce made her nose run.

She choked it down. She'd emptied her goblet but was desperate to wash away the pepper flakes searing her tongue. Aurelie leaned across the pushy fellow and seized his drink. She gulped half its contents at one go, only to cough in surprise as the clear liquid burned a second, even more incendiary, path down her throat. Not water.

Far from being offended, he grunted with approval. "Spirited girl, aren't you? Not at all what I'd expected from a lubber."

She couldn't mistake the tinge of scorn, but Aurelie was sputtering too breathlessly to challenge it. "What...what was—"

"Mother's private reserve." The Skoeran closed one eye and tapped the side of his nose. "More where that came from, Your Highness—you stick close to me." He swigged the rest, smacking his lips.

Aurelie stood up. "And you are?" Her voice came out shakier than she liked. Between the fiery spices and the liquor, her head was spinning.

The light eyes opened wide. "Plank me for a mannerless fool. Hui Inglis, First of the sailing vessel *Splinter*, at Your Highness's service." He stood and snapped off a salute, then seized her arm. "Let's promenade." His brisk air made it a command rather than an invitation.

Aurelie stretched her legs to keep up. She couldn't think how to extricate herself from a man so determined to parade his prize through the room. Even when he paused to speak to an acquaintance, Hui kept a firm grasp on her arm.

Diplomacy, she reminded herself. Best not offend her hostess's son. Especially when Aurelie's job included mending relations between their countries. She kept her mouth closed in a tight smile so as not to admit any more of the spicy Skoeran tidbits Inglis kept trying to feed her.

Other women, she noted, seemed flattered by the First's attention, whether to their plate, pearls, or person. Like his mother's, those light eyes calculated the worth of the goods on display, rendered an internal verdict, and moved on.

Inglis seemed a popular sort; guests sought his opinion on topics from weather and trade to fashion and politics. But his true passion, and that of his closest friends, soon became apparent. They shared a mania for sport. Three men arguing about crag-climbing routes halted their tour of the room for quite a while, as did a discussion ranking those of Dorisen's competitive step-racers not recovering from broken legs.

Aurelie stood, shifting from foot to aching foot in her tight shoes. Her neck itched. She scratched it surreptitiously. Her escort didn't notice her fidgeting. He was droning on about iceboats. "*Sea Wolf,*" he told a group of adoring young beauties. "Fresh crew, plenty of talent. They'll make the eight."

One red-haired girl with a band of emeralds blazing around her head dared to contradict him. "*Hirondelle's* helm told me they were sure to narrow her point deficit and qualify ahead of *Sea Wolf* for the finals."

"An iceboat crewed by women?" Hui Inglis's lip curled. "Isn't *Hirondelle*'s patron the same idiot who sponsored *Iceflash* two years ago? I heard she lost a fortune."

The redhead's cheeks flushed. Aurelie looked down to spare her embarrassment. Green light flared in the corner of her vision. The emeralds or the headache returning? She closed her eyes and willed it away.

"That rig's a show act, not a serious contender, mademoiselle," Inglis said. "Waste of talent, girls crewing iceboats. Why risk your pretty fingers to frostbite and worse? That's what brothers and sweethearts are for. Though women do make some of the fleet's best navigators," he added gallantly.

"And captains, and helms," Aurelie thought she heard, but Hui galloped her out of earshot before she could be sure.

An older man hailed them over a plate of scallops in a seaweed broth. "So what d'ye think of *Woolyworm*'s chances?"

Hui snorted. "*Gargouille*, you mean? Superstitious nonsense, that nickname."

Aurelie couldn't agree with him. She wondered whose stupid idea that had been, treating a dangerous Fae as a sporting mascot. Names had power. Gargouilles were even deadlier than dracs, though fortunately rarer. They must not live in Skoe. In Jocondagne, naming a vessel *Gargouille* and racing her anywhere in the country would be like shouting "Here, kitty, kitty" to a tiger.

"As you say, First." The man didn't argue, but he didn't repeat the name, either.

Inglis sneered at his caution. "That old tub has needed a refit for years, and with the current timber shortage..." He rolled his eyes in Aurelie's direction.

She hardly noticed. A large, loud group had drawn her attention to a corner of the room. Guests surrounded a cluster of boisterous young men and one or two women wearing red jerseys and gold caps with a dragon emblem picked out in red beads. Aurelie frowned when she recognized a gargouille's likeness. Under the caps, the iceboat crew's faces had been painted gold to match, like jeweled idols come to life. The effect was dramatic, and also strange, since the skin paint blurred the uniqueness of each person's features into the same gilded mask.

Why, then, should her eyes return to one man in particular, finding familiarity in his stance, the set of his shoulders, the considering tilt of his head?

He turned. Gray-green eyes met hers, and recognition sparked between them. Garin! The air left Aurelie's chest as if a suck-breath had stolen it.

Hui Inglis swung round to follow her gasp of surprise and swore under his breath. "Woolies, here?"

Fortunately, Aurelie was not required to answer. She needed to remember how to breathe. In, out. So simple, so impossible. Her insides tumbled; her skin tingled. This time, it wasn't liquor but impatience that set her whole body on fire. She willed her friend to cross the room and speak to her.

"Been at sea awhile, eh, Inglis?" The older man licked broth off his spoon. "Word on the wind, their new patron took *Fleur de Glace* apart for her wood and scoured the northern fleet for prime riggers."

If the man had more gossip to impart, his listeners disappointed him. At top speed, Hui towed Aurelie toward the woman dressed in crimson and gold who stood in the center of the room chatting with the Alsinhalese ambassador.

"Good evening, Ambassador." Hui dropped Aurelie's arm like a hot poker and seized Captain Inglis's sleeve. "Tell me you didn't take on *Gargouille*."

"Hoist chain, son," the blond woman said. "We'll discuss it later."

"But, Ma—"

He sounded, Aurelie thought, like a child unhappy with his Midwinter gift.

Captain Inglis patted her son's hand and smiled at Aurelie. The expression didn't reach her cold eyes. "Later, I said."

Aurelie took advantage of Hui's sulking fit to curtsy deeply. "A pleasure meeting you, First Inglis. Ambassador, Captain Inglis," she gabbled. Picking up her skirts in both hands, she swept across the floor as fast as her tortured feet would carry her. But when she elbowed her way into the group of iceboat riggers, Garin had gone.

CHAPTER 5

Garin

The gold paint itched. Cheap pigment mixed with grease, it smelled like sulfur and made my eyes burn, but I couldn't wipe it off until I'd finished spying on my employer. Though another rigger claimed credit, the costumes and makeup had been my idea. Those of Captain Inglis's guests who might know Garin Deschutes wouldn't see him in Gar the Woolie. Except my parents, and they'd arrived late and left early, careful not to give me away.

This party was an unexpected chance to get inside the Inglis town house. So far, I'd wasted it in the blue salon, stuffing my face with our host's excellent seafood and listening to that fool Neff yap about Princess Aurelie. *Too flat, too plain, too dull.* Dull? He had never spoken with her, that I knew. And, yes, her gown was simple, compared with other girls' getups, but it suited her. No show filly, this princess, foofy ribbons in her mane, oiled hooves, all that. A racehorse, Aurelie was.

And brave! On her ownsome in a room full of possible enemies but a smile on her lips, even if it wasn't her best one, the one that snuck out when you said something funny and caught you both by surprise. This one wasn't bad, a court number, serene. Princess Aurelie's real smile could make a person spend half the night lying awake, trying to think of amusing things for the next day. A younger person, say, who didn't know how fickle girls could be.

Another reason I liked the Jocondagnans' plain dress was that it made it easy to spot them coming and stay out of the way. I'd already scouted their guesthouse, spoken to a couple of their armsmen and chair porters. Netta hadn't traveled with the princess; someone would have mentioned a blind girl in the party. So Aurelie and I would talk when I was ready. Which might be never, considering how she'd plastered herself like a limpet to Hui Inglis's arm. How could the princess be fooled by him? I'd expected her to see past the First's rank and mark him for the callous, arrogant, shallow...filthy rich, good-looking son of a councillor he was.

I ate some shrimp and cursed the gold paint for making my eyes water. But I knew the minute she recognized me. A change in the air, like smelling rain in the wind. Oh, I could have—should have—kept my back turned, so she wouldn't be sure. But I was too glad. Glad and proud that she hadn't fallen for the disguise, proving my good opinion justified. Smart girl, that Aurelie. My best friend, once upon a time, when we were children. Before the war made us both grow up in a hurry.

It was worth the risk to see distant politeness sharpen to her most imperious look, *Come here, you*, even if I wasn't going to obey. Hui

Inglis hadn't gotten that look from her, or the secret smile, either. He wouldn't, if I could help it.

So I'd better do what I'd come here for, besides getting a look at the princess and downing several plates of devil squid so hot the fumes would have stripped varnish. The chef's best dish, in my opinion. He'd made it often when he cooked for us, before my parents' last run of bad luck.

Yet another reason to stroll out of the dining salon. Nonchalant. An invited retainer, out for a breath of fresh air. Nod at the footman like a guest with a little too much beer inside him. *Head's along here? Thanks.* Down a side corridor, look both ways, up a flight of stairs, right past another footman flirting with a maid. Slack job of keeping curious partygoers from the town house's private rooms, but I'm hardly going to report the poor lubber to Inglis, now, am I?

Bedroom, bedroom, man's sitting room. The captain's husband died last year, so this must be the son's. Dirty boots on the floor, animal heads staring from every wall, their glass eyes empty. Quite the sportsman, our Hui. Travels to foreign lands, sees beautiful, exotic creatures, shoots 'em, stuffs 'em, and hangs his bathrobe off their antlers. Another sitting room, crimson and gold (a theme, here?), a woman's slippers beside an armchair, more promising, I'd say, and behind the silk tapestry...yes!

Cozy little office, geraniums dripping down a balcony that faces the harbor, bet the view's a stunner in daylight. Feminine but not frilly, more flowers on the desk, three good seascapes. One of them my aunt painted; the frame's exactly the same size as a blank spot on the wall at my parents' house. Why *do* you hate the Deschutes so much, Captain? Or is it admiration that you covet our family's chef, our paintings, our trading partners, our voice on the council?

Strongbox bolted to the floor, no key I can find. Pity. A drawer full of ledgers, wish I had all night, but there's only time for a quick skim. Should have come earlier; guests leaving already, farewells drifting up from the courtyard below. Hurry, hurry.

I raced through the ledgers without finding the records I was searching for: Inglis's accounting of her joint venture with my parents. The goods were stored in our warehouse at D-dock: lengths of woolen cloth; spices from cinnamon to mustard; tea leaves, coffee, and cocoa beans; and delicate porcelain cups for serving the expensive brews. All awaited distribution to the most exclusive shops in Dorisen and abroad, too, once the treaty was signed. Bales and bundles, crates and chests, a profitable sale would restore my family's fortune, unless Inglis had found a way to cheat us. My father fully expected her to try. Hence, my employment as a Woolie.

I'd decided she must keep the records I wanted at the firm's office by the docks, when I found a slim book slipped between two others. No page titles, no headings to the transactions. All outgoing, it appeared, cryptic abbreviations and amounts. Large amounts. *6 c-ptr, r-t; 2 Jk crw, whs vst.* Payouts, maybe? Was this why the council deliberations went her way so often? It was a puzzle for later.

From down in the courtyard came a burst of drunken singing. Neff shouted, "Gar, hey, Garboy! Where'ye at?"

The rigger sounded stubborn enough to wait until I showed. Not out of any great affection; he'd think I'd found a better class of brew and was enjoying it without him.

I left the office as I'd found it. One glance down the hall told me the footman's watch had changed. A new man stood on the top step, whistling. I ducked into Hui's sitting room and fortune smiled: another balcony. It would be an easy jump to the garden wall and a convenient trellis, but I heard voices coming up the stairs. A man and a woman argued softly, the way people do when their house is crawling with guests. I crouched on the balcony just outside the door, hoping that the trailing geraniums and darkness would screen my gaudy outfit from the courtyard below.

"…told you to engage the princess, not that Burgida creature." Captain Inglis, laying down the law.

"Who, the redhead?" Hui, defensive.

"Absolutely off limits."

"I hardly spoke to her. Anyway, that Jok girl was eating from my hand; she'll trim out nicely, for a lubber. But what's this about *Gargouille?*"

"New opportunity."

"But, Ma, you said *I* could pick—" A door shut and cut off the conversation.

Moments later, I was slapping the rigger on the back. "Bunk time for you, Neff."

"Sailing the sweet salt sea," he bellowed, hitting only half the notes and blasting us with his pepper breath.

A waiting porter grinned, teeth white in the torchlight. "Two coppers says yon crewman takes the last step-way on his scuppered a—"

"Sure, sure," I interrupted him. "We'll beat you to the docks and collect." Princess Aurelie was stepping outside, hadn't the fool seen? She didn't deserve to hear that kind of language.

All the way down to our barracks, Neff sang and I stewed. So Captain Inglis had set Hui's sails in Aurelie's direction. Well, the First could chart the course, but it'd be an ill wind that brought him to shore. I'd warn the princess—as a friend—that the Inglises couldn't be trusted. All I needed was proof.

CHAPTER 6

Aurelie

"Where'd he go, puss?"

Amber eyes stared back at her. Aurelie snuggled deeper into the window seat and leaned against the cool glass. Fog had descended in the night and was lifting, grudgingly. Between rows of slate-roofed warehouses, a sliver of harbor glimmered deeper gray in the dawn light. Tied to the docks, the ships wore wisps of veil, like shy brides.

The cat nudged Aurelie's fingers. She scratched its chin. "I looked everywhere," she said. "Poof. Tricksy as a Fae." Long whiskers twitched; a purr rumbled in the cat's throat.

Aurelie opened the instrument case and took out her flute. Enjoying the wood's satin feel, she lifted it to her lips and blew. Softly, at first, delicate as the rising fog, the notes of a mountain ballad trickled out. Aurelie closed her eyes. She'd often played this tune for Netta and Garin and Loic. The drac loved her music. He'd sit so still he almost disappeared, letting Netta braid his hair into lutin twists. The melody—or the memory—worked its magic. Disappointment eased.

They hadn't spoken, but she had seen Garin. He was here in Dorisen, not at sea with his family's ships. She might meet him again today, or tomorrow; the negotiations would take time.

A faster tune followed the ballad, notes chasing one another like goats skipping from rock to rock. Beside her, the cat's full-throated purring stopped and his back went rigid. Still playing, Aurelie peeked through her lashes.

The ears flicked, the hindquarters quivered.

Cats were awfully moody creatures. They could be wholly present one minute, and the next...slinking along the floor after dust motes or spiders. Aurelie hoped it wasn't another big hairy one, like Elise had surprised in the washbasin the previous night. Aurelie squinted. Nothing, until she favored her left eye.

Oh.

The gray cat was stalking a lutin. An ugly one, the squishy, squashy body topped with giant bat ears and a shifty expression just visible through tufts of hair. Aurelie brought the tune to a close, set the flute down, and reached for a pair of boots, in case she needed to stomp in a hurry. But these two appeared to be old adversaries. Just as the cat pounced, the Fae ducked and rolled, tweaking the furry tail as he slid under the chamber door. The cat yowled in disappointment, then sat down, extended one hind leg, and licked with great concentration.

Aurelie rocked back against the window, struck by a new thought. Unlike animals, few people perceived the Fae's true forms under the illusions and invisibility they could wear like a suit of clothes. That's why lutins loved parties. From the cover of a crowd, they'd spill drinks on new coats, rip expensive lace, and unravel seams at the most inopportune moments. But Aurelie hadn't spotted a single one at Captain Inglis's supper or in the street on the way. If lutins weren't common here, and gargouilles were so rare their names could be used in sport, the Fae must not care for Skoe's climate or landscape. Or something. She'd ask Garin. If she could find him.

Like a hound tied to a tree, Aurelie's thoughts kept circling around his disappearance. Why had he worn that costume? Where had he gone last night? And why had he left without greeting her? Though their countries disagreed, she didn't like to think that her old friend might now consider her an enemy. They needed to talk. She frowned as she wiped her flute clean and put it away, wishing she had Netta's gift for gossip. The day they arrived, her friend would have heard all the talk of the town and known how to interpret it.

"More invitations, Princess Aurelie." Elise breezed into the room. She carried a tray laden with crockery, a couple of the hard rolls and dried fish that Skoerans called breakfast, and a stack of colored envelopes. Hard on her heels followed the two Skoeran modistes with bolts of fabric and stacks of pattern cards. Aurelie wished she could remember their names. By now, it would be awkward to admit she'd forgotten. She'd ask Elise later.

"Good morning, Your Highness," they chorused.

"And to you," Aurelie returned the greeting. "Do we have time for dressmaking this morning, Elise? I thought to attend the first diplomatic meeting."

"Oh, the count left already, Your Highness." The maid poured a cup of the bitter morning beverage Dorisen folk consumed by the pot. She added a generous dose of honey and handed the steaming cup to Aurelie. "He said that First Inglis would be calling on you shortly." A sly glance measured the Skoeran women's reactions. They looked suitably impressed, and the maid continued. "He's offered to show you the city, and I'm to accompany you." This last with a bounce of excitement.

"Oh." Aurelie tried to summon a matching enthusiasm. "First Inglis seemed very well connected," was the most positive thing she could say.

"For a lubber," the shorter dressmaker muttered, then smiled in apology. "Did you know he hailed from Jocondagne, Your Highness?"

Aurelie shook her head.

"He and his mother arrived here a few years ago. She married right off, into one of Dorisen's oldest families," the woman said. "A bit high-handed, some say, old Inglis appointing his new wife captain before she'd worked through the lower ranks, but the woman's not lost a hull yet."

"Her husband adopted the lad and taught the pair of them to sail like Skoerans. Except for her hair and those light eyes, you wouldn't know they were born off-island." The taller woman unrolled a bolt of fabric and held a length to Aurelie's face. "Not peach," she concluded, and tried another. "Perhaps the green?"

"Very nice," the other modiste said. "What do you think of this style, Your Highness?"

While the shorter Skoeran took notes, Aurelie expressed her opinion of the various pattern cards, fabrics, and trimmings. Elise sorted the envelopes. "Formal supper, informal supper, musicale, a fireworks display this evening, step-race. What's a step-race?"

"You might send regrets for that one, Your Highness," the note-taker ventured.

"Why's that?"

"Step-races last for ages. Unless someone loses his footing and falls, there's nothing much to watch."

Her countrywoman nodded agreement. "Like fishing tournaments. Hours of boredom, unless you're competing."

"How about iceboat racing?" Aurelie asked.

Both women brightened. "Now *that*"—one rapped her knuckles on the table—"is a sport worth watching. Do you have a favorite, Your Highness?"

"Never heard of it before last night," Aurelie admitted.

"No?" The Skoerans drew shocked breaths.

"It's a northern pastime, originally," the tall one said, as if this defect in Aurelie's education must be remedied at once. "From up in the Sleeve, a long channel between two islands. It freezes over by mid-fall, so Sleeve traders use freight sleds to transport goods over the ice. One man hoisted sails on his sleds, and the innovation led to sport."

Aurelie tried to picture it. "So iceboats are more like skates than ships?"

"Aye. Masted and rigged like ships, but with frames instead of hulls, and iron runners."

"My sweetheart took me once," the shorter woman said. "Ooh! We flew."

"Dangerous, the speeds they reach," the other said. "There's no good way to stop an iceboat except by dumping wind."

"Aye, but spills make the races exciting."

Elise pouted at the fanned invitations. "No one invited the princess to one of those."

The tall Skoeran chuckled. "The season hasn't started yet. Not cold enough for the race routes to freeze over. Besides, the trading fleets are still gathering in from summer routes. The iceboat patrons won't finalize their crews until they know who's staying in port for the winter."

"Really?" Aurelie put down her cup and nibbled on a roll. "I saw a crew at the supper last night. Red jerseys, gold caps, with a red, er, dragon." She wouldn't say the iceboat's true name out loud.

The two women traded silent glances. Intrigued, Aurelie floated a tidbit of gossip like a lure. "Captain Inglis is their patron, I believe."

"If anyone can tame that beast, it's Inglis," the tall woman said.

"She'll need her luck." The short one flicked her fingers in a warding gesture. "*Gargouille* killed half her crew last race."

Elise echoed Aurelie's horror. "The dragon *ate* them?"

"In a manner of speaking," the woman said. "Wind shifted, and she smashed into a cliff along the final stretch of the course."

The other Skoeran noticed Aurelie's distress but misinterpreted the cause. "I'm sure Jacinthe Inglis won't have any trouble. Her son's a competent officer."

"Hui?" Aurelie almost snorted out loud. She wasn't worried about him.

"So First Inglis will pilot his mother's iceboat?" Elise asked.

The other two women turned expectantly to Aurelie.

"I don't know," she said. "He didn't seem too pleased last night."

"Ah." Once again, nods were exchanged, while Aurelie wondered about the implications. Mother and son didn't agree about iceboats, but did that hint at a bigger rift between them? If Aurelie toured Dorisen with First Inglis, would it cause problems for the negotiations?

No, Count Sicard had accepted the First's invitation on her behalf; it must be all right. Even if all she wanted to do was march into *Gargouille*'s crew quarters and yank Garin out of that red jersey. No friend, whether speaking to her or not, deserved to crew on a cursed vessel. Hadn't he heard about the iceboat's reputation? How could she warn him? Where was he?

Hui Inglis answered her question. "*Gargouille*'s crew? In the barracks behind dry dock, most likely." The Skoeran gave Aurelie a speculative look. "You follow iceboat racing, Your Highness?"

"It sounds exciting." Aurelie pushed her hair out of her eyes and tried not to pant too obviously. The First's idea of a city tour involved climbing more steps than she could count. Until the Skoeran dressmakers had completed walking costumes in the local mode, Aurelie's unfashionably long skirts excused some of her slowness. She'd also hit upon the idea of asking her guide about the nearest point of interest whenever she or Elise needed to catch their breath. The maid's freckled face was scarlet with exertion, and Aurelie could feel a matching heat in her own cheeks. She welcomed the cool, moist sea air against her face. And this was autumn! How did the Skoerans manage all these steps in the heat of summer?

"We can visit her," Inglis said.

Aurelie yanked back her wandering thoughts. "Who?"

"*Gargouille.*" His booted foot tapped impatiently. For today's expedition, Hui Inglis had shed his dress blacks for a yellow coat and scarlet neckerchief, over brown trousers and glossy boots. "Any boat racing under our name needs to be solid. My mother thinks we can salvage the old frame, but I'd like to inspect it myself."

"If you like." Aurelie tried not to sound too eager. After a scant few hours in the First's company, she'd learned that he liked making the decisions. Perhaps it made him a good officer; she wasn't qualified to say.

Elise coughed discreetly. When they turned, the maid fingered her collar. "Spider, monsieur."

"What?" He looked down and blanched.

Aurelie thought Loic would have enjoyed the way Hui Inglis jumped around, slapping himself. When they were younger, the Fae had often dropped insects down his friends' backs. A lutin's trick, they'd complained. Couldn't dracs do better?

"Is it off? Did I get it?" Hui said.

"Yes, monsieur," Elise said.

Aurelie pretended she hadn't noticed that the haughty First was afraid of a spider smaller than the ones who lived in the guesthouse baths.

"Those striped ones spread disease, you know."

"Ah," Aurelie said. She hadn't noticed any stripes.

He straightened his neckerchief. "I-dock's this way." He charged down the closest flight of stairs.

Elise sighed. "Don't your feet hurt, Your Highness?"

"One more stop, Elise," Aurelie promised. Her feet were fine, her calves and thighs less happy about all the climbing. "After we see the infamous iceboat, perhaps First Inglis will feed us."

"Fish again," the maid said glumly.

Dry dock wasn't a dock at all, as Aurelie had expected. Instead, Inglis led them to a large stone warehouse, from which came the knocking of hammer blows and a man's fine baritone belting out a bawdy song. Their escort slid open the wide, barnlike doors. The strong smells of paint, glue, and sawdust poured out.

Inside, a good twenty people, including the singer, labored over a wooden frame. Up in a loft that spanned half the building's length, more workers crouched over an expanse of red canvas. No scarlet jerseys and gold face paint today; many of the men had stripped to the waist, and the women wore practical tunics and leggings. There were trestle tables covered with gear, barrels and tools, strings of colored signal flags, long iron runners stacked together. No Garin. Like fog, disappointment filled Aurelie's chest.

"Sorry, mam'selles. This area is closed." A man met them, hands extended in a polite shooing motion until he recognized their escort. He snapped to attention. "First Inglis," he said loudly. "Welcome."

The hammer beats paused, then picked up, faster than before. The singer stopped mid-note. Aurelie was sorry. She liked the rollicking tune, though the words weren't really suitable for polite company.

"We'll show ourselves around," Hui Inglis told the man.

"Aye, First." The man backed away, and Aurelie noticed that his skin was covered with wood shavings, like a pollen-dusted bee.

Elise sneezed once, then again and again. She fumbled for a hand-kerchief. "Glue," she muttered. The smell didn't bother Hui Inglis; he strode across the warehouse, easily navigating the maze of timber.

"Why don't you wait outside, Elise? This shouldn't take long," Aurelie said. Especially her part of it, since she hadn't found Garin and she didn't care about iceboat construction.

Inglis, unfortunately, was both interested and knowledgeable. He walked along the frame, calling one worker after another to defend some aspect of its construction.

Aurelie held her own handkerchief to her nose against the strong odors and the dust and picked her way along the wall clearest of paint and glue pots. When she reached the back of the warehouse, she fol-lowed the sound of raised voices and the scent of grilled fish. A door stood open in the corner.

"...*he* doing here?" a woman's taut voice said. "A free hand, I was promised—"

A man's voice answered, the words inaudible.

"Aye, but—"

Another murmur.

The woman's voice sounded somewhat familiar, but Aurelie defi-nitely knew the man's. Though it was deeper than she remembered, she'd heard those same soothing tones before. Of the four of them, Garin was the levelheaded one, tempering Loic's wilder ideas when Aurelie's pride and Netta's faith in her friends would have sent them willy-nilly after the drac. Aurelie's pulse leaped. Her feet carried her in a rush through the doorway and into the paved yard beyond.

Wearing a stained apron over ragged tunic and trousers, Garin stood beside a stone grill, flipping fish steaks with a long-handled scraper. The change in his companion's expression warned him. He turned, neat as a cat, and saw Aurelie.

Delight, hurt, suspicion—expressions flashed across his face so quickly that Aurelie wasn't sure she had read them correctly. Then, most confusing of all, a kind of blank, dense good humor settled over his face, making it even more foreign than the gold paint had, or the years, turning the boy she remembered into a man. Not as tall or handsome as Hui Inglis, dark-haired and green-eyed, Garin had never stood out in a crowd, until a person noticed how capably he completed any task he set himself. At present, that appeared to be cooking for the iceboat crew.

Aurelie regretted the impulse that had sent her charging into the yard before she had decided what to say, how to act. However she'd imagined their meeting again, it wasn't with the reek of glue in her nose.

Garin saluted her with the scraper and a vague smile. "Hullo, pretty lady. Mind the firewood—meant to stack that this morning." He kicked a pile of small logs out of Aurelie's way.

One rolled in the wrong direction, under her skirts. She hopped, slipped, and grabbed his outstretched arm to right herself. He caught her waist and swung her around as if this were the first step in a dance the two of them had practiced a hundred times.

In childhood, Aurelie had trusted Garin to catch her when she leaped into the river, to boost her into a pine tree's upper branches, to fight at her back when Netta and Loic attacked with willow switches for swords. Though she didn't recognize the expression Garin's face wore, her body knew the arms that held her.

She relaxed. Strong and pliant both, Aurelie balanced on her toes, poised for the next step. It seemed her partner felt the same. The hand with the scraper shifted to support her hip. His other hand lifted to slide her tumbling hair from her ear. Garin's body curved over hers, and his lips followed his hand, whispering, "Don't know me."

His breath tickled. Her whole body thrilled as his thumb pressed her parted lips, preventing her from answering. She tasted lemon and fish and warm skin, and then he straightened. Setting both hands on Aurelie's hips, Garin lifted her off her feet and plunked her onto a stool next to the grill. He looked her straight in the eye as if they'd never met and smiled with rude good humor. "Fish 'n' flatbread, pretty lady?"

"Uh…" She licked her dry lips and closed her mouth on mounting anger. How dare Garin act the fool with her? But the heat in her blood chilled as she read a warning, as much in his stiff movements as in the words he'd whispered. Elbow jerking like a jointed doll, Garin wielded the scraper. Aurelie wanted to cry for that brief, fluid moment when they had almost been dancing.

"Your Highness!" The woman Garin had been speaking with bowed deeply. "We met last night, at Captain Inglis's supper. Helm Burgida, at your service."

With a start, Aurelie recognized the redhead who had crossed Hui Inglis. She looked older in the dark green tunic and leggings, her striking red hair confined to a single plait down her back. But even in the plain light of day, the air seemed to shimmer around her, as if traces of the salon's candlelit opulence lingered in her hair, on her clothes. Or, as if…Aurelie squinted, and froze. The human shape overlay quite a different one.

Helm Burgida was a Fae.

CHAPTER 7

Aurelie

Aurelie's right eye showed her an attractive woman whose face was a bit too angular, her frame too wiry, for true beauty. Aurelie's left eye saw a dragon. Not a gargouille: much smaller, fortunately, than either that giant bronze beast or the more common river drac. Jointed wings, like a bat's, folded along a scaly green body. The head was wedge-shaped, with a long muzzle and a hollow dished out in the broad forehead between the two sorrowful eyes.

Aurelie had observed the same melting expression in calves, in puppies, and once in a day-old fawn. This was a thousand times worse, because the muddy green eyes weren't animal but human. Except the Fae weren't human, and rarely sad or sorry. Aurelie clutched the stool's cane seat, her fingers biting into the weave. Pity surprised her out of a lifetime's caution. "But," she blurted, "how did—aren't you—"

"*Helm* Burgida?" a derisive voice overrode her question.

Aurelie swallowed her words, grateful for once that Hui Inglis didn't mind interrupting other people's conversations. As she realized what she had almost betrayed, sweat prickled along her upper lip. Despite the Fae's woeful air, her claws and teeth promised danger. Why hadn't Garin warned her? Aurelie shot him a questioning look and met the same blank stare.

The First lounged in the doorway, scoffing. "Even if she passed the tests and apprenticeship, who'd hire a woman to steer his ship?"

The Fae calling herself Burgida bowed again. "Another woman, First Inglis."

His cheeks flushed an unbecoming red. "My mother hired you?"

"We reached an agreement this morning," Burgida said. "I'm to helm her iceboat this season."

Hui Inglis's fists clenched. He straightened from the doorframe with a violence that had Aurelie tensing on her stool. The helm didn't move, but the air around her bloomed with danger, a rusty tang that Aurelie tasted in the back of her throat. Her stomach turned.

When Loic smelled like that, she, Netta, and Garin had learned to leave him alone for a while. And he'd been a baby, with hardly any magic. Aurelie didn't know what this dragon-woman might be capable of, but she didn't want to find out in a high, walled courtyard where Hui Inglis blocked the only exit. He couldn't be aware of Burgida's true nature; Aurelie didn't believe a competent ship's officer would dare to treat a Fae like a flunky.

What had possessed the otherworldly creature to put herself in this situation? Except for the melusines, Aurelie hadn't heard of Fae pretending to be mortal for more than a few hours at a time. This one must have passed for years to earn a helm's rank.

Yet Inglis bulled toward her, stupid with anger.

"The flatbread smells delicious." Aurelie jumped off the stool and helped herself to a knife from the table next to the grill. A poor weapon, but better than nothing if the Fae attacked. "Baked with garlic and rosemary, yes?" she babbled, trying to draw Hui Inglis's attention to herself. "They make it that way in the mountains near Cantrez, where my mother was born. We'd spend summers there, on Grand-mère's farm." She chose one of the small loaves cooling on the rack and sliced it in two, then held out the bread so Garin could flip a seared fish steak onto each piece.

"Cantrez?" Hui stopped short.

"You've heard of it?" Aurelie shoved a piece of bread and fish into his hand.

"Aye." The First spat on the ground.

Before Aurelie could react to the insult, Garin took two lurching steps from the grill. His scraper waved between Burgida and Inglis, and the First had to retreat or risk getting fish grease and charcoal smeared across his yellow coat. "Hot sauce or lemon, pretty lady?"

"You'll address her as Highness," First Inglis snarled. His free hand cuffed Garin's ear.

Aurelie tensed, but Garin dropped against the stone grill, managing to make it look accidental that no part of his body touched the banked coals. Her silent apology didn't penetrate Garin's blank expression. "Lemon, thank you," she said. "And another for my maid Elise, if you'd be so kind."

"Crew slop," Inglis sneered.

Aurelie's temper, stressed already by his rudeness, snapped. "Then I'm sure it's good enough for you, *First*," she said, leaning on his title.

She took a big bite of steaming, flaky fish and the garlicky bread underneath. No spices, no sauces, just honest food, perfectly cooked, and about time, too. She chewed and swallowed. "Unless First is a courtesy title?" she said with poisonous sweetness.

He couldn't object to the insult, since she'd posed the slander as question. A muffled cough behind her told her that one other person, at least, appreciated the distinction.

"No, Your Highness," Inglis said. His dignity was spoiled by having to lick fish juice off his hand before it could drip onto his polished boots.

"Nor helm, neither." Garin held out his hand for the knife. Reluctantly, she surrendered it. Burgida had slipped away; Aurelie wouldn't need it anymore. Garin sliced another loaf. "Lotsa tests, the officers take. Makes my brain hurt, thinkin' on it."

"I'm sure it does," Hui Inglis said sourly. "Princess Aurelie, if you're ready?"

Aurelie nodded. Garin gave her another helping of fish and bread wrapped in a worn cloth napkin. "For your maid. Highness."

"Thank you." All her attention was focused on the spot where their fingers met. Not quite a squeeze, nothing so definite as a caress, but the light pressure filled her with warmth. He turned back to the grill, humming under his breath as if she'd already gone.

She'd found him. She even thought she understood why he didn't want her to acknowledge him. Princesses usually didn't recognize lowly crewmen and cooks; both Burgida and Inglis would have wondered at it. Curious, though, that Garin should be keeping company with a Fae. Not to mention working for a rival family's iceboat crew.

If Aurelie remembered correctly, Garin's parents were merchants like the Inglises and just as prominent in Skoeran society. Garin must have a good reason for hiring out. Had his clan's fortunes suffered during the war? Not an easy question to ask; Garin had his pride, too. How else could she find out? Again, she missed Netta. Her friend would know exactly how to discover the truth without hurting anybody's feelings.

In thoughtful silence, Aurelie followed Hui Inglis's stiff back through the warehouse and out the sliding doors to rejoin the waiting Elise.

Crew slop or not, the First had finished his meal almost before Elise had taken one bite. The Skoeran recovered his good humor by relating several tedions anecdotes from his most recent voyage. Things were always breaking on a boat, it seemed, and needed to be fixed with the tools and materials on board, which were never precisely suited to the job.

"Excuse me, First Inglis," Aurelie inserted into one of his infrequent pauses for breath, "does Dorisen have a library?"

"Certainly, Your Highness." He sounded affronted, as if she'd accused his capital of lacking covered sewers, or any other benefit of civilization. "We'll pass it shortly, up two step-ways from the university's main lecture hall."

Behind them, Elise made a small, unhappy noise. Even before the iceboat warehouse, the maid's enthusiasm for the city tour had flagged. As they'd approached the step-way that led down to their guesthouse, her pace had picked up, like a horse that scents its stable nearby.

Aurelie wanted to visit the library, but not with Hui Inglis looking over her shoulder. She cast about for an excuse to be rid of him. "I'm afraid we'll have to leave the remaining sights for another day, if I'm to sit in on the afternoon session."

"Afternoon session?" The Skoeran sounded puzzled.

"The treaty negotiations," Aurelie reminded him.

"They don't need *you*, do they?" he asked, and again Aurelie heard him telling Burgida that it was a waste of talent for girls to crew ice-boats. His own mother was a captain. Why did he have such a low opinion of women's capabilities? She hoped, for their sakes, that none had to crew under him.

"I trust Count Sicard completely, but I like to know what's in the documents I sign." She curtsied. "Many thanks for this delightful and instructive morning."

"You're most welcome." He smiled, and Aurelie understood why the Skoeran women found him so charming. "Until soon, I trust," he added. "Fireworks tonight, down at the harbor. My mother's partners are sponsoring; they should put on a good show. You'll attend?"

"I believe we received an invitation," Aurelie said, and curtsied again.

As she descended to the guesthouse, her head buzzed with plans. She needed information about Skoeran Fae and Dorisen's trading families and iceboat racing, to start with. She'd leave Elise to soak her sore feet, and hire a box-chair to visit the library.

But when they reached their rooms, Count Sicard waited, his ruddy face creased in anxious lines. "The negotiations are not going well, Your Highness." He paced across the floor of Aurelie's sitting room, boards creaking under his weight. The resident cat watched his progress through half-closed lids. "Captain Inglis has demanded the most extraordinary concessions regarding timber allotments. Both the Alsinhalese ambassador and I find them unacceptable. This morning, I regret to say, our hostess flew into a rage, accusing us of sabotaging the talks and, worse, attacking Skoeran convoys on the high seas."

"Is that true?" Aurelie asked.

"No, of course not."

"But we confiscated some of their hulls at the Lumielle breakwater, didn't we?"

"Well, yes, when war was first declared. But they've been returned, and we've initiated no attacks since the truce was declared. Unfortunately, Captain Inglis has convinced herself—and many of her fellow councillors—otherwise. If you'd attend the afternoon session, perhaps your presence would moderate her behavior."

Aurelie's lie to Hui Inglis, back to bite her. "Why should she listen to me?" Aurelie said. "The Inglises don't seem to care for anyone's opinions but their own."

"The captain seems to, ah, entertain some hopes regarding her son," the count said, delicately. "The two of you enjoyed spending time together at the supper last night, and his attentions today were not unwelcome?" he finished, as Aurelie frowned.

"Frankly, monsieur, I'd rather not marry Hui Inglis," she said.

"He didn't, ah, that is, your chaperone..." Eyebrows raised, the count glanced at Elise, who shook her head.

"We had a fine time," Aurelie said. Except for Hui hitting Garin. "I just don't think we'd suit."

"But for a day or two?" Her adviser spread his hands in polite inquiry. "At least while the negotiations are in such an unsettled state."

More lies. Aurelie sighed. But the count had only asked her to butter up the Inglises until the treaty could be signed. She probably wouldn't have to work very hard at it. Hui, at least, was capable of flattering himself; she had only to smile and hold her tongue, and he would think her in complete agreement. Of course, she would also have to delay satisfying her own curiosity. That was a small sacrifice, for her country's sake.

She forced her lips into a false smile, no doubt the first of many. "I'd be honored to attend, monsieur."

"Splendid."

When the worry lifted from the count's face, Aurelie knew she'd made the right decision. That didn't mean she had to enjoy the results.

CHAPTER 8

Aurelie

Alone in her box-chair, Aurelie brooded on the afternoon's events as the porters carried her away from the meeting rooms, down toward the guesthouse. During the session, Captain Inglis had been brusque to the point of insult to all the participants except Aurelie. Under that lacquered helmet of fair hair, the woman had skin like cowhide and a tongue to match. Whatever had possessed the other Skoeran councillors to put her in charge of the treaty talks?

Aurelie squinted through the window slot into the gathering dusk. Oil lamps glowed in windows and over doorways, though Dorisen's streets were otherwise unlit. A few people trotted past the box-chair, hurrying homeward for their suppers, most likely. The approach of night didn't slow her porters. Two lanterns fixed to the roof of the box-chair cast halos of light fore and aft. In their watery glow, the porters marched easily down the step-ways.

Until the first explosion.

"Plank me!" At the loud booming noise, the man in front stopped short, causing the rear porter to slew the box-chair sideways.

"Watch yer step," the second man growled.

The chair bobbled. Aurelie put her eyes to the slot. "What's happening?"

"Trouble at the docks," the lead man said. "Hear that?"

Another dull boom echoed up the crater's sides, followed by the crackle of smaller arms.

"They attacking?" The second porter sounded more resigned than afraid. "Councillor said the truce wouldn't hold. Cursed Joks, can't trust 'em farther nor I can spit." He hawked up a gob of phlegm and demonstrated.

The box-chair shook. Aurelie shrank against the bench. *Cursed Joks?* Did they resent carrying her? Should she try and escape? It couldn't be her father's forces attacking, not while she was in Dorisen working for peace. The Alsinhalese, maybe? But they, too, had sent a representative. Had the Skoerans other enemies? And which two-faced councillor had spread such a vile rumor? It must be a mistake.

"Shift stumps, man," the first porter said. "We'll ship this load, get to a station, case there's fire."

Aurelie clutched the frame as her box-chair heaved like a ship in a storm. With little care for their passenger's comfort, the porters charged down the stairs. When they reached the guesthouse court-yard, they heaved her out of the box-chair. She swayed on the pavement, trying not to cry from her fear and the rough handling. If the fighting started again, what would happen to her party? Except for a pair of armsmen, their crew had stayed aboard ship rather than come into town. Less provocative, Count Sicard had said, and Aurelie agreed. Dorisen's council had stationed city guards at the guesthouse gate, but they owed no loyalty to the Jocondagnans.

"Sorry, mam'selle." The lead porter jerked his thumb at the other. "We're fire line, see, to keep the ships 'n' warehouses covered."

Aurelie nodded, not trusting her voice. At least they hadn't left her at an upper level to make her way down alone in the dark. Or worse, dumped her in the harbor as a "cursed Jok." She pressed a coin into the man's hand.

"Right kind of ye, mam'selle." More box-chairs rattled into the courtyard. Count Sicard tumbled out of one.

"Aurelie!" he called, his voice rich with relief. The informality startled her, until she realized that, ever the diplomat, the count had avoided using her title in order to protect her. He must have heard the same tale from his porters: a sneak attack and Jocondagne to blame.

The box-chairs were jostling for the courtyard's single exit when the sound of cannons firing made all those present cover their ears and run to the shelter of a shed's overhanging roof. The sea breeze carried a sulfurous reek.

"Harbor guns?" a rough voice said.

"Nah," another man answered, sounding doubtful. "More like—aww."

A huge orange chrysanthemum bloomed over the city. Each slender petal folded into a lick of flame that kissed the dark before melting into nothing.

Ssssss. Boom! A thunderclap split the sky. This time, a giant blue and green spiral unwound, rippling to earth like a knot of celestial snakes.

The porters burst out laughing. They slapped each other on the back. "Over the yardarm, man."

"Had *you* spooked, dinnit?"

Count Sicard chuckled weakly.

"The fireworks," Aurelie said out loud. Her knees gave way, and she sank, mindless of her long skirts, onto the ground.

Doors flew open; lodgers and servants ran out to see the spectacle. *Bang! Bang! Bang!* Plumes of white light waved overhead. Yowling, the gray cat shot across the courtyard and disappeared inside the guesthouse.

"Isn't it splendid, Your Highness?" Elise appeared beside Aurelie. The maid hopped from foot to stockinged foot on the cold stone. "As good seen from here as any old reviewing stand."

Aurelie hugged her arms across her middle. Her stomach still felt queasy, as if she'd swallowed too much fear. "Who invited us, again?"

"The D-something family. Desfleurs? Desamis? The sponsors, anyway."

"Deschutes?" Aurelie croaked.

"Yes, that's right," Elise said. "You met them?"

Garin's family. "No," Aurelie said, and tasted brimstone with the lie. Smoke wafted past her upturned face as a hundred ruby pinwheels spun into oblivion. Garin's command echoed in her brain. *Don't know me.* Lies upon lies, and what would she have said to his parents? Just as well the diplomatic session had run late.

A question stirred in the back of Aurelie's mind. "I thought First

Inglis said his mother's partners were sponsoring the fireworks?" She was asking Elise, but a porter answered.

"Aye, mam'selle. That's a new deal."

"Talk of the wharves," another man put in. "Captain Inglis don't take partners, her usual run of business."

"Hauls her profits on a short line," a third agreed, rubbing his fingers together. "Whoo, d'ye see that?" A burst of green, red, and blue sparks crackled into acrid smoke.

"Between Deschutes' hulls and her investment, they'll make a killing," the first man said.

"Good timing for Deschutes' too; they'd a run of mortal bad luck, lately."

"Bad luck or bad judgment? *He's* all right, but that wife"—the porter shook his head—"shiny brightwork, but not much ballast to her hold. These fireworks, f'rinstance. Generous of the lady, but not too business-wise, spending her profits afore they're counted into coin."

"The Deschutes hadn't hooked up with Inglis, they'd be sellin' hulls to cover their old debts."

Fascinated, Aurelie listened to these working folk discussing the affairs of Dorisen's most prominent families. As Lumielle's citizens did hers, no doubt. "What about their children?" she heard herself asking.

"Bit of a dandy, that Hui, but a sound head on his shoulders. He'll rise far in the fleet," her porter predicted.

"And the Deschutes?" she said.

"Dunno 'bout them."

"Girl and a boy, wasn't it?" another porter offered.

"Nah, just the one boy, but he can't be much help to his folks. Fostered off-island, I heard. No rank in the fleet, any road."

"Seems I recollect—"

But what the porter recollected was forgotten when an immense *BOOM* was chased by a grinding, creaking roar. A hungry sound, Aurelie thought, and shivered. From the direction of the harbor, red-blue flames shot into the air. They started much lower than the previous displays, barely clearing the rooftops behind the docks.

"Dud fuse," a porter said. The others cursed.

From an upper story of the guesthouse, a woman leaned out a window and shrieked. "Fire! Fire on the docks!"

As if in response, bells clanged all along the waterfront, a brassy counterpoint to the leaping flames. "Hoist chain for yer stations!" a porter yelled. Dropping their box-chairs, the men ran from the courtyard, leaving the Jocondagnans gaping after them.

"Excellencies!" The guesthouse night-man opened the door and motioned frantically. "Come in, come in. Along to the dining room, if you please."

Inside, Aurelie and her party found a scene of controlled chaos. Servants ran down the stairs, carrying armfuls of stiff white fabric from the attic.

"Fire law says everyone helps with the buckets and pumps," the night-man told them.

Count Sicard drew himself up. "You can't mean to endanger our princess."

"Got two arms and legs, don't she?" The man looked frightened rather than angry.

The guesthouse cook laid a meaty hand on the count's arm. "Canvas cloaks and bonnets made out of old sails protect us pretty well," she said.

"I don't mind," Aurelie told them. "But my maid must have shoes, and we'd better wear leggings; these skirts will slow us down."

"Sure, sure—go get 'em, sweetheart," the cook said.

Elise scampered up the stairs while Aurelie reassured her adviser. "Dorisen seems well-prepared for fire. We could take some of their ideas back to Lumielle. And most of the buildings here are stone, aren't they?" She appealed to the cook, who seemed the calmest person present. "What's to burn?"

"Ships and goods, mam'selle." The woman pulled on a floppy canvas bonnet. "Gotta keep the sparks off the docks and outta the rigging, that's the main thing."

The guesthouse's residents put on the capes and assembled in the dark courtyard. Aurelie thought they all looked ghostly, shrouded in white.

"Remember," the cook said. "Gotta keep yourselves wet down, like so." She demonstrated by emptying a bucket of water over Count Sicard's bonneted head.

Aurelie held her breath as Elise did the same for her. It made the bulky cape heavier and the bonnet clammy, but she could see the sense of it. A hot rain of ash and embers dropped from the sky. As instructed, Aurelie pulled a wet strip of fabric over her mouth, which helped. At street level, the air was breathable, though smoke swirled in gusts, stinging her eyes.

The roaring sound had quieted; the bells still clanged. As the Jocondagnans squelched in a line after the cook, the night-man bringing up the rear, more people flooded down the step-ways. The street filled with wet, pasty-looking creatures, as if the drowned had risen from watery graves and marched on the city. Aurelie shook off the unpleasant image.

Ants, she decided, were preferable. Industrious insects, passing buckets of seawater, instead of leaf bits, along their endless columns. She wasn't afraid until she reached the harbor and saw the size of the fire. A row of ships burned, some distance along the inside curve of the shore. Smoke billowed out of a building at the head of the same dock.

"D's gone," a man shouted at the cook from an oxcart full of wooden buckets. "They're pulling back to F-dock."

The cook nodded. "We'll aim for H, wash 'er down," she shouted back, and turned to her crew. "Take a bucket and follow me."

One by one, each person collected a bucket and tramped toward the docks, merging into the swarm of white-caped figures. In moments, Aurelie was just a pair of hands in a chain, passing buckets of seawater to other hands to splash over furled sails, masts, bowsprits, decks, hulls, dock timbers, carts—anything that might burn. They started close to shore. As more people rushed down from the city's heights, heeding the bells' summons, the fire-lines extended until each finger of dock was carpeted in white.

When Aurelie's bonnet dried out, she stuck her head in a bucket. When a spark burned through to Elise's arm, Aurelie doused her white cape again. The wind blew off the sea, pushing the worst of the smoke from their position on H-dock. Still, the air tasted thick and sour. Aurelie coughed behind her mask. Unused to such hard labor, her arms tired quickly. She kept on, turning and lifting. More people came; she knew because she didn't have to reach as far to pass the heavy buckets. Blisters rose and popped on her palms, stinging with every splash of saltwater.

The night became a blur of bells and heat and smoke. Salt crusted on her cloak and stiff fingers; heavy buckets hit her in the stomach. Reach, pivot, shove. Next bucket. For hours and hours. For the first time, Aurelie was glad Netta hadn't come to Dorisen. At least her friend had been spared this ordeal.

Once, distant white figures yelled and retreated from a dock. Two ships lit up like fireworks, and it seemed the whole city groaned in dismay as they burned to the waterline. As the blaze consumed a merchant's precious cargo, the air filled with the exotic scent of charred spices. Bucket by bucket, Dorisen's residents fought back.

"Here, you girls. Other side." The guesthouse cook pulled Elise and Aurelie out of their line and into a different one, empty buckets returning to be filled, and that was a little better. Still, the breath rasped in Aurelie's throat. Exhausted tears washed soot down Elise's cheeks. They must be equally freckled tonight, but it wasn't funny, not really, when Aurelie realized with a pang of despair that she could see Elise's face clearly. The fire had found something new to burn, and the nightmare would never end.

She was wrong. The sky continued to brighten, first in the east, and then all around. Sullen light filled Dorisen's stone-walled bowl; the sun glowered red-orange behind a pall of smoke. Suddenly, it was morning and the fire was done.

"Come, my chicks." The cook took empty buckets from Elise's and Aurelie's cramped hands, and then the three women sat on the dock and cried together. "Saved H-dock, blessed if we didn't." The Skoeran wiped her broad face on her sleeve, smearing the caked soot.

Aurelie sniffed and blinked. Black specks clung to her lashes; her eyes felt full of grit, and she didn't know whether she could find the strength to stand. Flecked with ash and floating pieces of charred wood, the greasy water pushed against the pilings. Other people shuffled past them or lay where they were, rolled in dirty canvas capes.

"Can we sleep here?" Elise said.

"Folk do, what live in the heights," the cook said. "But the guesthouse isn't so far. Pot of coffee, bit of a wash, you girls be up 'n' dancing."

"No dancing and no coffee," Aurelie groaned. Stiff in every joint, she hauled herself to her feet and held out a hand to Elise. "A bath and bed."

"Indeed." Count Sicard stood behind them, his eyes red from smoke, but courtly as ever in his filthy cape. He offered his arm to the cook. "Today, madame, a cup of your Skoeran brew will be most welcome."

"Aye, get along with ye." The woman mustered a smile. Wearily, they all marched back to the guesthouse.

In their absence, the gray cat had done his part to protect them. Aurelie found the evidence on her coverlet: two large headless spiders and a lizard's tail, likewise detached. "Bravely defended, puss." She scratched the purring animal's chin, then gathered the sorry collection in a handkerchief and tossed it out the window. She collapsed into bed and directly into a dream where she, Loic, Hui, and the decapitated spiders chased one another through a maze of fire.

Loic cackled. "Did I get him?"

"Off me!" Hui's handsome face twisted in disgust.

The spiders, being headless, said nothing. Their furry legs simply scuttled faster, carrying Aurelie with them into the smoke.

CHAPTER 9

Garin

The house stank of burned wool. I'd come through a side door, past the heap of capes dripping sooty black blotches onto the stone floor. It was a risk, going home, but any servants not asleep should be packing their bags and hoping to find employment with a luckier family. Down two corridors and up a flight of stairs, I didn't pass anyone but a sulky lutine. She was occupied snapping the heads off the daisies arranged in a tall glass vase and didn't spare me a squint. I left her alone. Why chase her? She'd only come back later and smash the vase. We were going to need every last coin the house and its furnishings would bring at auction.

I found my mother in her parlor, which I had expected, and Father, too, which I hadn't.

"Garin." Mother stood up from her writing desk and opened her arms. A person who didn't know better might have mistaken her for a society matron who'd spent the night dancing and risen late to sip coffee and answer her correspondence. She wore a blue silk wrap and a pair of feathered slippers, her hair bundled under a scarf. The coffeepot was there, and a biscuit crumbled on a china plate, and a pile of letters next to a silver opener.

But the papers were covered in angry PAST DUE and NO FURTHER CREDIT stamps. Fresh bandages covered the blisters on her hands, and ashes had sifted out from under the head-scarf to dot the back of her wrap.

If I said anything, I'd cry like a baby. So I hugged her. She smelled like lilac and soot. On this evil morning, everything in Dorisen smelled like soot. Me, Father's old coat, the bare floor where I sat, since my clothes were too dirty to touch the velvet seats.

"What news, son?" My father stood by my mother's chair, one hand on her shoulder. To give strength or draw it? He looked as if years had been added to his account with every hull that burned.

"Are we quite ruined, dear?" Mother asked, almost playfully. She must know. Bowed shoulders said they both did. Still, Mother sought to spare me grief by acting as if it didn't matter.

"Yes," I said, before my throat closed, and I had to stare hard at the rug. Not the keenest head for business, my mother. But brave. The bravest woman in Dorisen.

The silence stretched. Father stumped over to the coffeepot and poured me a cup, cold and tarry. I slugged it down, realizing I hadn't drunk anything for hours. Or eaten, either. Not that I was hungry.

Father sat down at last. "We've the two ships still out."

I turned my empty cup around. "If they've had a good run, we can salvage the smaller repair yard, with the apartment in back."

A tiny sigh escaped my mother. "And the hulls? Can't we send them out again in the spring?"

"No. They'll both go to Inglis. Her share of the cargo was in our warehouse. Whatever we can raise from the house will go to settle that debt." I set the cup down, wanting to grind it into the saucer. But we were too poor for me to smash valuable crockery like a cranky lutin.

"I blame myself," Father said. "My idea, going into partnership with that vulture."

"No, dear." Mother perched on the arm of his chair and tucked her hand into the crook of his arm. "We all agreed. You can't spear sharks from the dock when they swim in deep water."

"It seemed like a good plan." Father's chin sunk onto his chest. "As partners, we'd see one set of books, and if Garin could get to the figures she showed for her taxes"—he thumped his fists together. "The money's not coming out of the air!"

I hated to add to their troubles. "Maybe it is."

"What?" They both stared at me.

"Inglis hired a Fae to helm her iceboat."

"A Fae?" My mother's forehead wrinkled. "Like a lutin, you mean?"

"Not a lutin, more like a drac. I've told you about them."

Father leaned forward. "Why would she want one? And what could she offer that would tempt such a creature? They don't have much to do with men, as I understand it."

"Not usually, no. They mind their business, and we mind ours." Except sometimes.

"Wait—didn't a drac blind your little friend?" Father said, remembering that one exception. "Does this Fae understand that you've recognized him?"

"Her," I said. "And no, she doesn't; I've been careful. Knowing Inglis, there's probably a threat involved." I thought of Burgida's sad, sad eyes and couldn't believe she was crewing for Inglis except under duress. If the princess hadn't interrupted our conversation...but remembering the way Aurelie had looked at me and how it felt to hold her was another fist to the gut. I had to keep my mind on saving my family, not the princess. Especially if she was mixed up with that arrogant—

"Son." My mother's gentle voice. "Do you want out of there?"

My fists clenched, but that hurt. I spread my blistered hands on my knees. The Woolies weren't bad. It was realizing that my labor put money in my enemy's pocket that made my working hours so hard. And that when my family needed me, I wasn't with them.

"No, Mother. Now more than ever, I've got to find out what she's up to. If she's got one Fae working for her, why not more? A matagot, a couple of suck-breaths, or a White Lady?"

My parents looked confused. I kept forgetting; they hadn't lived in Jocondagne, hadn't seen what I saw or heard Madame Brebisse's stories. "Matagots are treasure Fae, I guess you'd call them," I explained. "They take the shape of big cats, apes, rats, or foxes. To catch one, you stake a chicken at a crossroads on a moonless night. If a matagot comes for it, you stuff the Fae into a sack and carry it home without looking back. That binds the matagot to serve you. Every morning, more gold appears in your treasure chest."

In ordinary Dorisen, it sounded unbelievable, but my parents nodded, trusting me to know. "What price the creature's aid?" Father asked. A merchant's question. No one gives something for nothing.

"Your soul," I said. "Unless you can pass the matagot to someone else before you die."

Mother pursed her lips. "But wouldn't anyone greedy enough to trap one in the first place find it difficult to give up? No matter how much treasure they'd gathered, they'd always want one more morning's worth."

"Exactly. And White Ladies—actually, I don't think they travel very far from the place they're born, or made. Created." I'd seen one once, in the woods near Cantrez and never mentioned it to the others. We hadn't played near that cave again, but those bony fingers sometimes reached for me in dreams.

Mother frowned. "Jocondagne sounds like a frightening place. How do people live there, prey to creatures most of them can't see?"

"The Fae don't interfere much in our world. Except for lutins, like we have sometimes, they don't care for human settlements." I don't know why I defended the place, or the Fae, considering what one had done to my friend. No aid without price, but only Netta had paid for Loic's gift. What happened when my account came due? Or the princess's? I reminded myself I wasn't thinking about her. "And they can be beautiful, like the Fée Verte or a troop of farfadets dancing in a meadow on a summer's night." It hurt to talk. Better save my breath for what needed to be said. "No, I'll keep on with the

Woolies, find out what's what. I just wanted to make sure you were all right."

"Better, after seeing you," Mother said.

"I'll go down to the docks again later," Father added. "I'd like to know where the fire started."

"A dud firework, I thought." Mother turned to him. "Didn't it light the warehouse and burn outward from there?"

Father's mouth twisted. "Probably."

Our warehouse had a slate roof. A dud should have burned itself out without reaching the cargo inside. Why hadn't I realized?

I felt like I'd been carrying a lutin disguised as a log. Just when I didn't think it could get any heavier, the weight doubled. Did Father suspect sabotage? If so, he wasn't saying, for Mother's sake, until he had proof. My mind raced. The only warehouse that had burned to the ground last night belonged to the Deschutes, along with the ships tied in front. C-dock had lost two hulls, but most of Carnwell clan's ships were late returning this year and not expected for several days. Accident or design? Who hated us that much?

"I'd better go." When I stood up, each separate bone ground in its socket, another painful reminder of the previous night.

My mother embraced me, grime and all. "Shall I—" her hands fluttered. "Is there anything you'd like me to keep out from the auction, sweetheart?"

I thought I'd steeled myself to our losses. The fire hadn't killed anyone, thankfully. But even though we'd extinguished it at the docks, the beast's hunger hadn't been satisfied. Its red jaws still gnawed, sharp teeth tearing my liver.

What did I truly care about in the room upstairs? Clothes? Skates? Throwing knives, climbing gear, all could be replaced. I'd never spent much time in that room, anyway, between fostering for years with Aurelie's family in Jocondagne, then spending the winters since in the warehouse or repair yard with Father and summers with the fleet. My hammock in *Far Venture* must have burned with the hull, ashes in the water.

There was a box of boy's treasures behind a loose wall panel: fish-hooks, shells and beach glass, an owl pellet embedded with a tiny skull, a lutine's golden hair wrapped around a twig. Nothing I needed; I could leave it for the room's next occupant. Except for two items. "The model of *Far Venture*," I said, "and the miniature on the dresser."

"Of course." Mother smiled. "We saw her at the supper the other night. She's grown into a beauty, your little princess."

"Not my princess."

"Have you spoken with her?" my father asked.

I shrugged. "What's she going to say to an iceboat cook?"

They had no answer, and so we parted.

Plodding down the step-ways, I couldn't stop thinking about Aurelie and the shadow I'd seen in those dark eyes. Had the war put it there? Or losing her mother? We'd heard that Queen Basia had died, but at the time I couldn't find a smuggler willing to carry a message as far as the court in Lumielle. And I hadn't wanted to embarrass the princess by sending a Skoeran's condolences in the diplomatic pouch with our council's demands. To be truthful, I also hadn't been that eager for Captain Inglis to find out we were on friendly terms. The less the councillor knew about me, the better I liked it.

Especially if she wanted her son to marry the princess. For

Aurelie's fortune, or her title, or her royal blood? All of the above, probably. One seat on the council had never satisfied Captain Inglis; she wanted her family to rule Skoe forever. Or so my parents worried, and I hadn't seen anything to convince me otherwise. Still, whatever his mother's ambitions, no woman with half a brain deserved to be shackled to that windbag Hui.

"Hey, Gar-boy. You coming with us?"

Outside *Gargouille*'s shed, half a dozen Woolies milled by the door. A rigger was tapping a barrel of the pitch we used to seal cracks in planking. The sticky liquid oozed into a bucket.

I scratched my head. "A caulking party?"

"No." Neff dumped an armload of torches next to the door. "That fire last night? We found out who set it."

"Fireworks accident, I thought."

"Joks." Another rigger folded his arms across his chest. "A nest of 'em, I heard. Came for the treaty talks, they *said*, but all along they meant to burn Dorisen to the ground. Couple of 'em spotted on D-dock before the fire."

"That's right." Neff trimmed a lantern wick with his knife. "And two others here yesterday, trying to steal our secrets so they can build their own."

"We don't ship 'em out of town, they'll set our shop afire next."

The *Jocondagnans*? I needed to speak with Aurelie, make sure the rumor wasn't true. It made no sense. Her country needed this truce as much as we did. If not us, who'd buy their timber, grain, and food? Who'd bring them trade goods, fabric, and spices? Why would they attack the one family in Dorisen who knew and liked them?

Anger chased a spurt of fear. I wanted to punch the rigger's lying face, but common sense stopped my hand. I couldn't take them all. My brain ticked on, a cold machine. The entry from Inglis's secret ledger flashed in my brain. *2 Jk crw, whs vst.* Two Jok crew, warehouse visit. Had the captain paid them to set the fire? Had some trouble-maker done it on his own?

Either way, the Woolie crew were strictly followers. Someone had pointed them at Aurelie, and my quarrel lay with that person.

Helm Burgida had come up behind me. Her amused voice cut into the crew's angry growls of agreement. "Oh, come now," the Fae said. "Spies? You mean that slip of a girl with First Inglis yesterday? I doubt the little lubber could tell a square knot from a bowline. And the other one couldn't have seen much more, for sneezing."

"Due respect, Helm," the navigator said, "this is men's business."

I smelled rust and lightning and backed away from Burgida. I rubbed my jaw. "Dunno 'bout that, but I've had enough fire to last me awhile. You fellows've got it covered. I'm for a wash and my twenty winks."

"Say, Gar," Neff said, "how 'bout we bring you a plump Jok pigeon to roast for supper?"

They all laughed. It was hard work to smile vacantly and sham-ble in the direction of the bathhouse. When I rounded the corner, I ran for the princess's inn. Matching me step for step was the Fae Burgida.

I'd figure out what to do with her when we got there. Until then, I needed all my breath.

CHAPTER 10

Aurelie

"Please, Your Highness, wake up."

A hand shook Aurelie's shoulder, sending darts of pain down her arms. She spit out a mouthful of covers and opened her eyes. Sunlight pressed against the curtains, tinting the room a deep amber. Elise's apron hung crooked against her skirt, and wisps of hair straggled out from under her cap, as if she had dressed in a hurry.

"Another fire?" Aurelie coughed. Sand lined her throat.

"No, Your Highness. First Inglis is downstairs with Count Sicard. Urgent, monsieur says. You're to dress and join them as fast as may be."

Aurelie pushed herself upright, stifling a groan as the movement twisted her aching arms and back. Elise had worked as hard as she, and the maid wasn't complaining, though she moved with less than her usual sprightliness. She poured from a porcelain pot, and Aurelie gulped the tea, an herbal flavor that refreshed her parched mouth.

"Hands, please." Elise unwound the bandages from Aurelie's blistered skin, dabbed ointment on her palms, and wrapped fresh linen around them. Then she helped Aurelie dress in one of the new Skoeran walking costumes, the green of spring leaves. "Sets off the red lights in your hair very nicely, Your Highness," the maid said. "Lace mittens over the bandages, and a body wouldn't know you'd spent all last night fighting that awful fire." She combed Aurelie's tangled hair and plaited it.

Aurelie grimaced at the mirror. "If you have a matching veil to cover my bloodshot eyes, I might almost believe you."

Elise sniffed. "Anyone without them means they hid inside, away from the smoke. Badge of honor, cook says."

"I'll keep that in mind. Let's see what brings the First to our doorstep, shall we?"

"Trouble, Your Highness." In the downstairs parlor, Hui Inglis bowed over Aurelie's lace mittens. He, too, wore gloves today, she noticed. Red rimmed his light eyes. A model citizen, by all accounts. So why couldn't she help comparing him to his countryman?

Garin might have visited, now that she thought about it, to make sure she was safe. Or had he assumed that Aurelie would stay away from the danger? That she'd grown up into a ninny, cowering in her room while Dorisen burned around her ears? Funny how physical danger wasn't as frightening as the other kind. Fire she could fight with a bucket, same as the next person. The need to secure the peace weighed more heavily, and it was a burden fewer could shoulder. Still, a friend would have come. They really didn't know each other anymore, if Garin could think her a coward.

"Your Highness?" Hui Inglis stepped back, and Aurelie realized she was glaring at him.

She perched on a settee next to the count. The shorter skirts swished around her ankles. "What kind of trouble, First Inglis?"

"Apparently, there's talk going around the docks, Your Highness," the count said. "Two Jocondagnan men were reported skulking around the warehouse before it burned."

Aurelie went rigid. "Not the place we visited yesterday?"

First Inglis preened. "Considerate of Your Highness to concern yourself with our property, *Gargouille* included. No, the warehouse that burned was above D-dock, though it also, alas, housed a goodly portion of our cargo, through a partnership of my mother's with the Deschutes family. *Splinter*'s safe at I-dock, thanks in no small part, I understand, to your own valiant efforts at H."

Aurelie sat mute, transfixed by self-blame. How could she have been so selfish? Garin's family had lost their warehouse and cargo and ships. Little wonder he hadn't come calling. If she could help...a loan, perhaps, from the funds they'd brought. Or even a friendly word, if he'd take it from her.

"Yes, yes." Count Sicard glanced at Aurelie. "First Inglis has been generous enough to warn us of this brewing unrest and offers a safe haven at his mother's residence in the heights until the misunderstanding is cleared up."

"Box-chairs are outside," Hui Inglis said. "We'll send men back for your things, but in the meantime, Your Highness, may I suggest an immediate departure as the most prudent course?"

"Leave the guesthouse?" Aurelie said. She couldn't seem to focus on what the First was saying. How Garin must be suffering! He'd never want to watch fireworks again.

"A temporary measure," Hui Inglis assured her. "After last night's unpleasantness, tempers may be running a little hot." He smiled at his own joke.

Two quick raps on the door and Elise burst into the room. "There's a crowd of rough men four streets down," she gasped. Her freckles stood out against her skin. "With torches, coming this way."

"Thank you, Elise." The count stood, dragging Aurelie with him. "Let us go, Your Highness. It appears we owe First Inglis a great debt. We're most grateful, monsieur, to accept your mother's invitation."

"The pleasure's ours," the Skoeran returned, holding the door open. "I've instructed the porters to travel home on different step-ways, so as to draw less attention."

Aurelie felt as if her brain was splitting. Part of her remembered to paste a calm expression on her face, even smile at the guesthouse cook, as if escaping two steps ahead of an angry crowd armed with torches in the middle of the afternoon was nothing more than a minor nuisance. That part, call it the Heir, noted how First Inglis strolled into the courtyard, smiling like a fox with a partridge, while Count Sicard steered her toward the box-chair closest to the gate. Then another porter's intent gaze caught hers. With a heartbeat to decide, Aurelie waved Elise to the first chair and took the second for herself.

Another part of her fumed. She had helped fight the fire! How could anyone believe her countrymen responsible for such devastation? Did Garin think that? Had he heard rumors of treachery even before the fire, and that's why he didn't want her to acknowledge him? Because he was ashamed of her? All night she'd breathed smoke and hoisted buckets until her hands bled. They all had, all the Jocondagnans! She intended to tell him so. Very soon.

This chair's not following Elise's, the dispassionate part of her mind noted. Of course, Hui Inglis had told their porters to split up. He was smart, the First, and levelheaded in a crisis, although Aurelie couldn't find it in herself to care for him. Or trust him, as one of last night's porters had so picturesquely said, as far as she could spit. How curious that her mind and heart should find themselves at such odds. Illogical, even absurd, what she had done, and yet...

We've reached the harbor, not the heights. Her nose reported burned spices, tar, fish, and drying seaweed. Aurelie put her eyes to the viewing slot. Outside, the docks bumped up and down. A rather jouncing ride; her porters hadn't had this job long. But they should be well clear of the rest. She rapped, hard, on the roof. "Porter!" she called. "Stop the chair, if you please."

"In a moment, mam'selle," a smoke-roughened voice said behind her.

Aurelie's teeth clicked closed, narrowly avoiding her tongue. "Garin? Will you please tell me what this is about?"

The box-chair dropped with a crash to the dock. The door swung open and Aurelie tumbled into Garin's sooty arms. He looked a mess, but she didn't care. He was all right! Not burned, just weary and dirty, his hair matted with ash, like a bird's nest. Finally, they were together without a spying Inglis present. She wanted to fling her arms around him and bury her face in his neck.

But she restrained herself and was glad she had. Wouldn't she have looked stupid, considering how the Skoeran set her down as if she burned his hands. He stared at her, accusation in those gray-green eyes. "Did your people set the fire?"

Shocked out of speech, she shook her head.

"Sorry." He swiped at the dark streaks on her sleeves. "Had to ask."

Aurelie found her tongue. "May we talk now, since I've connived at my own kidnapping?"

"Rescue," Garin corrected, his face stern. "You chose the box-chair, didn't you?"

"Yes."

"Then get into the skiff, please. Your ship's at T-dock across the harbor, and we haven't bought much time. You found the oars, Helm?"

"Aye," a woman's voice said. "Casting off."

Aurelie swung around, hands on her hips. Her distinctive red hair tucked under a cap, Burgida slapped a mooring rope from its cleat. Ah, yes. There had to have been two porters, though Aurelie had only paid attention to the one in the back.

"Quick," Garin said. "I need to get word to your people." He hesitated. "Remember me to Netta, would you?"

"Certainly, the next time I see her. She lives with her uncle in Cantrez now and won't travel." With dignity, Aurelie stepped into the little boat and took a seat in the stern. If she had given Garin her hand, he'd have known that she was trembling. She'd ask herself later why it seemed so important to match his cool manner.

"Fair winds." Garin's foot pushed the small craft away from the dock. Without a backward glance, he walked away. Helm Burgida rowed. Wind ruffled the dirty surface of the harbor and teased strands of hair loose from Aurelie's braids. Ashes swirled away from the oars. The boat bounced in the light chop.

Shaking with disappointment and pent-up questions, Aurelie peered through her hair at the Fae, first with one eye, then the other. Woman, dragon. Woman, dragon. Very strange. At least it gave her something other than Garin's infuriating behavior to occupy her mind. "Why are you doing this?" she asked.

The Fae glanced at her. Woman. Dragon.

Aurelie blinked and wiped her face on her sleeve.

"Gar doesn't trust Hui Inglis," Burgida said. "Figured you'd be safer on your own ship, with your own crew. We bribed a couple of porters outside the inn, told them where we'd leave their chair."

Aurelie persisted. "But why are *you* involved?"

"Maybe I'd rather Jacinthe Inglis didn't get her claws into another innocent." The Fae hesitated, though the oars cut cleanly through the water. "And that Gar runs a deep game. I'm curious to see how it'll play out."

"What do you mean?" Aurelie hugged her knees. The wind's cold fingers feathered her hair. Had the Fae suspected they could see past her human form?

Instead of answering, Burgida shrugged. "And it can't hurt, Jocondagne's Heir owing me a favor." Briefly, she smiled.

Aurelie saw a dragon's teeth and controlled a shudder. "Thank you," she said. "I'll remember your kindness."

They rowed the rest of the way in silence.

CHAPTER 11

Loic

Humans lie. That's their nature. As well blame a fox for stealing eggs, a snake for slithering on its belly.

No, it's not their lies that trouble me; it's the *ingratitude*. Show them marvels, they'll take it for their due. Share your innermost self, and they forget you. Best friends one day, and the next—what's the quaint expression? They "grow up."

Only children believe in fairies, they're told, so they pretend they can't hear you calling, don't read the messages you send. Some don't even have the decency to say farewell to your face; they just stop coming.

But before my friends' desertion could wound me too deeply, my father announced that I was old enough to begin the study of magic, a grand undertaking better suited to the Fae world than an isolated river near an unimportant human town. I quit my former home without looking back.

It's disappointment that turns a Fae mean. Not all, of course.

Some of us rise above early slights or ill treatment to develop other aspects of our characters. Extensive practice may be required, but unlike humans, we immortals have plenty of time.

I devoted myself to my craft and had achieved no little degree of competence when curiosity prodded me into bidding my parents farewell and venturing the Door upon another mortal Where, another mortal When. I thought myself prepared for every contingency. While I'd been otherwise absorbed, three days—or three centuries—might have passed in the mortal world, rendering my former playmates dust and ashes, a memory on the wind.

So imagine my feelings to emerge into a gargouille's lair (unoccupied, conveniently, madame's table habits not being all one could wish in a host) and find myself near Jocondagne's capital. Discreet inquiries revealed that King Raimond ruled, with Aurelie his Heir.

Yes, *that* Aurelie! I'd last seen her as a gangly child, standing hip to hip with Garin, blasting toadstools off a log with my father's pistols. Not a bad shot, the little princess, but not as accurate as myself or Netta. Sweet Netta; of the three of them, she was the first to insist that I be pulled out of the bear trap and released into the river. Not that I couldn't have saved myself (which would have been more amusing), but that was my first experience with human kindness, and I craved more. Had I understood how sharply their cruelty could bite, I might not have put the ointment on their eyes or gotten to know them as individuals and considered them my friends.

Ah, well. None of us is perfect, mortal or Fae. I disobeyed my father in befriending the children and taking them the ointment he had made for my nurse. No need to lie to *her*—Jacinthe and I hated one another cordially, so she never questioned the many hours I absented myself without explanation. Deception came naturally, of course, to the human children. They concealed our friendship from their kind and mine, and we all had a grand time. At least, I thought so. But dwelling on the unpleasant past runs contrary to my nature.

My tail wags. I've chosen dog shape rather than invisibility for this inspection of Lumielle. A street urchin pats my glossy black fur, and I angle my neck so he can reach the sensitive spot behind my ear. Humans are clever about some things. Market day, for example. And sausages.

There's no taste quite as satisfying as a stolen sausage on a cold autumn afternoon. My ill-dressed companion agrees; he's already eaten more than his share. I permit the minor gluttony. The cart on rue Cabanis has many more, hanging in luscious strings to exactly the right height for snatching if one happens to be an athletic dog with a human child willing to provide a distraction. The vendor won't miss another three…or five.

And then I smell her. So useful, dog senses. Extracting myself from my accomplice's clutches, I trot down the street. The princess is climbing into a closed carriage. I pause in an alley, change into a sparrow, and—*flip, flap*—I flit into the carriage just before the door shuts and the driver chirrups to his horses.

Her astonishment delights me.

"Loic!" Her head falls against the cushion, lovely bronze skin fading several shades.

I resume my own shape, in tribute to our former closeness and as a compliment to her. Not easy, sitting upright on a swaying carriage bench when one's lower body ends in a lizard's tail, but for Aurelie I make the effort. One has one's pride. And also, sparrow throats are less well designed than a drac's for conversation. Though it's a moment before I answer. The most peculiar emotion threatens to overcome me. But, as one of the greater Fae, rather than a common lutin who must display his every mental process, I present her with a smile of gentle goodwill. "How do you fare, sweet princess?"

"Oh, well. You're so...you look older!" She gulps a couple of times. Not an attractive response, though I make allowances for surprise. She couldn't smell me coming, after all. An apology would be graceful at this moment, but humans are always thinking about themselves. Their short span of days, I fear, makes it impossible for them to take the long view as we dracs do.

"Jocondagne's at war with Skoe, did you know?" she continues. "We had hopes for a treaty, but there was a terrible fire in Dorisen, and they blamed us, and we had to leave in a hurry. Come spring, Father expects they'll attack in force."

As if human politics mattered to me. "What of Master Garin?"

Color returns in ugly blotches to her face. She twists her gloves in her lap. "His family lost their fortune, but he was fine otherwise. Last I saw him."

"And Netta?" If I didn't know better, I'd think those dark eyes accused me. Age has only enhanced Aurelie's unique intensity. I smile again to put her at ease.

"Netta's in Cantrez, at her uncle's farm."

"That's a pity," I say, and mean it. Disappointment burns like a gargouille's breath. No Netta? She and I had always teamed against Aurelie and Garin. Hardly a fair matchup, though the other two did their valiant best to keep up with us.

I strive for detachment. A drac is complete unto himself, viewing human company as a pastime like any other, to be enjoyed when the opportunity permits. Not needed for happiness, but certainly very pleasant. "You must come to a revel some night soon, my dear."

"A revel? I thought your father didn't allow—"

"My father no longer governs my actions. No other Fae would presume to dictate to a full-grown drac." Except, perhaps, for a gargouille, but the issue is moot.

"Oh, Loic." Aurelie reaches out to touch my arm as if she requires proof from more than one sense that I do, in fact, exist. "I'm the Heir. I can't leave Lumielle."

Rarely do her kind visit our world. Perhaps she does not understand the honor implicit in the invitation. Magnanimous as always, I give her the benefit of the doubt. "No one will notice if you're absent for a few hours," I assure her. "I'll fetch you from your chamber, all perfectly discreet."

"Um." Her confusion makes her look ten years old. A charming age for mortals.

Horse hooves and carriage wheels crunch on gravel as the vehicle glides to a stop. Briefly, I regret the coachman's skill. Flying off the bench to land in the woman's lap would be humorous, though hardly polite. Particularly when renewing her acquaintance after a span of years. "Look for me."

The door handle rattles. Aurelie puts her hand on the latch. I wink at her, and fade from mortal view. The princess can see me, but as far as the driver knows, she's the only one stepping onto the palace drive and breathing deeply of the crisp, cold air.

Delight fills me, undiluted, as I make plans to entertain my former playfellow. Together again, after all this time. Oh, this will be fun.

Chapter 12

Aurelie

Loic. In Lumielle. She didn't trust his world-weary air. Had he followed her, intent on mischief? After checking the bedclothes for frogs and spiders, Aurelie had slept uneasily, half expecting him to pop out of her wardrobe or slide under the door in a puff of smoke. No drac at breakfast, pulling faces behind her father's back. No Fae waiting in the carriage to ride out to the festival grounds, his unearthly beauty tying her tongue into knots. He hadn't listened about Garin; she couldn't tell him about Netta. And she couldn't worry about the three of them now. Aurelie pursed her lips.

Two-whee. Two-whee. She whistled the two descending notes and saw the huge sea eagle flying straight at her head. She braced her feet against the reviewing stand. Despite her intentions, at the last minute she flinched and crooked her arm over her hair.

"Elbow straight out, Princess," Master Austringer growled. "Paumera's an old war bird; got to give her a perch, not a target." The lanky, gray-haired man held Aurelie's right arm to the side, thick leather gauntlet uppermost. "Make a fist," the falconer instructed. "Here she comes."

The bird landed solidly on Aurelie's glove and clapped its wings to its sides. Aurelie staggered back into her instructor's arms. Though stringy, the king's falconer was stronger than he appeared. The old man supported Aurelie's elbows to keep her from falling off the reviewing stand and into the dried leaves that littered the festival grounds.

Eye to eye with the big raptor, Aurelie held her breath. She was awed by the intelligence in Paumera's golden gaze, the perfection of the bird's creamy feathers. Neck plumage ruffled as the bird shifted on the leather glove, then opened and closed a sharp-edged beak.

"Reward!" Master Austringer said. "Take the fish."

Aurelie's right arm dipped as she reached her left for the bucket. The falconer tucked a raw fish into her glove and Aurelie held it out for the white eagle.

Snap! Paumera lunged for the fish, snatching it from Aurelie's hand and downing it in one bite. Aurelie staggered, knocking her head against the falconer's chin. "Your pardon."

"Never mind that. Send her up again," Master Austringer said. "Quickly!"

Aurelie pursed her lips and whistled three ascending notes. The eagle's muscles bunched; her wings spread wide. Aurelie needed both hands to lift the bird high as Paumera launched herself into the air and flew north and west toward Lumielle's Tower Bridge, where the assistant falconer waited with more buckets of fish.

"Not bad." Master Austringer rubbed his hands together. In

approval or against the afternoon's cold, Aurelie couldn't tell. "See if she'll circle for you. Remember the *au tour?*"

"Yes." At her request, the falconer had been teaching her the commands for "up," "down," and "circle," in preparation for the Longest Night ceremony. The exercise gave Aurelie a reason to leave the palace every afternoon and escape from Elise's fussing over her clothes, the discussions of siege fortifications and tactics, the sober-faced advisers and men in uniform, each one a silent reminder of her failure.

Nobody accused her out loud of restarting the war. King Raimond had agreed, when she recounted the events in Dorisen, that Aurelie's party had likely been safest on a Jocondagnan vessel. Unfortunately, the princess's defection had infuriated Captain Inglis. Claiming an insult to Skoe's honor, she had persuaded the governing council against continuing the peace talks, and the Alsinhalese and Jocondagnan delegations had been shipped home like shabby secondhand goods. Which was all Lumielle had for sale these days without Skoeran ships to supply her merchants.

This winter, as the specter of war stalked the capital, Aurelie thought people needed to see the royal white eagles spreading protective wings over the city. It had been years since King Raimond had hunted with them, but the falconer thought some of the long-lived war birds might remember their training and respond. In a few weeks, they'd find out for certain.

Meanwhile, Aurelie and Master Austringer rode out of Lumielle every afternoon. They wove between the military supply wagons and crossed the River Sicaun to the parklike island to practice drills of their own. The command calls were only a few notes long, far less complex than those used to summon individual birds. Like its name, the *au tour* swung in a circle, from high to low and back up to the starting note. Aurelie whistled it as clearly as she could. To her enduring amazement, the bird tipped one wing and returned to soar in lazy arcs above the reviewing stand.

Master Austringer grunted. "Try the *plonger* command again."

"*Two-whee! Two-whee!*" Aurelie whistled. Talons extended, Paumera dropped.

A few curious folk had rowed over to find out what was happening at the festival grounds. Some cried out; others ducked under the reviewing stand's bare platform. Aurelie had trouble watching the bird dive at her. She slitted her eyes and hunched her shoulders. When the bird hit her glove, Aurelie's eyes popped open. She reached back for the reward. This time, she managed to hold still as the razor-sharp beak nipped the fish from her glove. "You beauty," Aurelie breathed. The eagle preened her breast feathers and gazed alertly at Aurelie.

"Now the *monter*," Master Austringer said.

With some reluctance, Aurelie whistled Paumera up and watched her fly away. The eagle's graceful flight and fearless eyes brought her thoughts back to Loic. No doubt the Fae lurked somewhere nearby, hoping to startle her as he had in the carriage. He could be watching this moment, as a man, beast, or bird. She didn't want to gratify his vanity by looking, so she concentrated on the sea eagle. One problem at a time.

"Try Montbrai, Paumera's mate," the falconer advised. "Those two were ever the best-trained. They haven't forgotten a trick."

"I thought the war birds had gone wild," a young woman said. "How do you get them to answer the whistles?"

Master Austringer grunted. "Been down here every day for weeks, reminding them what men are good for. Especially when the river freezes, the birds won't mind performing for their supper. Soon, this year. Cold's on the way—can't you smell it?" The falconer hummed a few notes. "That's Montbrai's call."

Aurelie whistled the phrase and laughed in delight to see another white shape lift from a treetop and fly toward her. "Look, he's coming!"

"Note-perfect," the falconer approved. The bird thumped onto Aurelie's gauntlet. With a twist of his powerful neck, he accepted a fish. Smaller than the female, this eagle's tail was barred with dark lines.

"*Monter,*" Aurelie said, and whistled the notes. She lifted her arms, but the bird refused to let go of the gauntlet. He clicked his beak, shifted his weight, and craned around Aurelie's shoulder to peer suggestively at the fish bucket.

Master Austringer barked a laugh. "He'll get another fish when he earns it. Try again, Princess Aurelie. Lower your arms after you've given him the signal. Montbrai's too haughty to let himself be dropped in the dirt."

Aurelie nodded. "*Monter,*" she said. As she whistled the command, she pushed the bird into the air. Her arms fell back toward the reviewing stand, and the eagle's wings unfurled. With an irritated squawk, Montbrai flew. Aurelie whistled the *au tour.* More swiftly than Paumera had, Montbrai sketched a cursory circle, then swooped to land on Aurelie's glove and claim his reward.

"Here's your fish, greedy guts," she said. The fish disappeared into the bird's beak. Aurelie had just time to whistle the *monter* again before the bird lifted from her fist and sped toward the bridge tower and the chance at more fish. "They're so different!" she said.

The falconer's weathered face creased in a smile. "Aye, Princess Aurelie. Must say, they've taken a rare liking to you," he pronounced. "House Pygargue knows its own. Their kind has protected yours for hundreds of years. It's how the ceremony started."

Aurelie stared out at the eagles. More birds had risen from the treetops along the river. They soared above the festival grounds, seemingly awaiting a turn to perform. "House knows House," she repeated softly. Her thoughts flew past the eagles to the river's mouth and over to the sea beyond. Who was watching over Garin's house? Could they tell her what had happened to him?

"If you wanted to bring them back to the castle mews after Longest Night, I think a few pairs would come," the falconer said. "Paumera and Montbrai, at least. Maybe more."

Aurelie shook her head. "If we have to, we'll put them in leashes and hoods. But until the festival, they may as well fly free."

"As you wish." Master Austringer tucked his hands under his armpits. "We've plenty of whitefish and more birds to remind of their place in the ritual, Highness. Call Orbec next; she sulks when she thinks she's been slighted."

At last, a task she could complete. For the moment, it was enough. Aurelie put thoughts of the war and Garin and violet-eyed Loic out of her head. She turned her face to the sky and whistled.

CHAPTER 13

Netta

A snowflake melted on my cheek. More delicate than rain, this first snow of the year, like the brush of an eyelash, a butterfly kiss.

Blindness had made me a connoisseur of weather. Soon the deep cold would close its fist around Cantrez, but so far the snow only tickled. I hugged my shawl to my shoulders and tipped my face to the sky, turning until I faced the wind head-on. A north wind, gusting. I fancied that before reaching me, it had passed through Dorisen and tugged Garin's hair on his way to the harbor, swept over the palace roof in Lumielle, and whipped the last leaves from the trees in the festival grounds where Aurelie trained with the sea eagles.

Mother had read me the princess's letters, expressing her disappointment at the failed peace mission, praising the falconer and the birds. The last letter, quite short, bothered me, mostly for what it didn't say. I was blind, not stupid. Or at least wiser than I'd been two years ago. Though I could no longer see, I listened. People's voices, I had learned, were less guarded than their faces. "What is she hiding?" I whispered.

The wind spoke to me, soft as a sigh. *Faaaaaaaae.*

My toes went cold in my boots. Two years, and not a word from Loic. My uncle's farm wasn't so far from the river. I admit to a secret wish, in those first dark days, that my friend might undo his father's curse. Never strong, that hope had faded. Perhaps I'd been mistaken, fancying that Loic and I shared a special bond. He might not care for me as I did him, but if he was in trouble, I needed to know. Was Aurelie trying to shield me from pain? Had something happened to Loic? As answers went, that would be dreadful, but it made my duty clear. Oh, let me be honest. More than duty, my *desire*. I wanted out. Out of Cantrez and out of my life as the seamstress's poor cursed child.

For two years, I'd kept to familiar places: my uncle's farm, the orchard, the market, the flower seller's home. Rosine and I had become close after it happened. Her son called me Auntie and climbed over my lap as if I were his own personal mountain.

I knew every voice in Cantrez: who loved me, who pitied me, who simply feared me, as if my unexplained affliction might spread, like the plague. No one but Aurelie and Garin knew that the river drac had taken my sight. I owed my friends the warning, but I had asked them not to relay the news to Loic. It wasn't the Fae's fault that I'd been careless with our secret. I couldn't bear to spread disaster to his family too, like a child who wipes her muddy hands on her playmates' clothes, so everyone goes home dirty. Then he disappeared and left me only memories.

After two years in this refuge, the thought of returning to Lumielle and Aurelie made happiness bubble through me. New tastes, new smells, new sounds, new voices. I wished I could fly and be there already.

"Netta!" My mother's voice, anxious. The door slammed. Her footsteps echoed on the front porch; the third plank creaked. "There you are dreaming again, and night coming on."

"You know darkness doesn't matter to me, Mother. Uncle wants his tea, you mean, and Orianne's buried herself in a book and won't answer."

"Your cousin tries."

"It's all right." Five steps, and I'd reached the railing. Beeswax and rose soap, my mother's scent, as recognizable as her face. I took her hand and let her guide us into the warm kitchen. "I'll make tea tonight, but Orianne's on notice. She'll have to do it or persuade Uncle to make it himself when we're in Lumielle."

"Lumielle?" A long, slow breath. "Travel will be difficult at this season."

"Aurelie needs me, I think." I squeezed my mother's arm. "And you, too. Especially since she lost Queen Basia. Madame Pevrel's an excellent housekeeper, but her fashion sense? As well ask Uncle to supervise the princess's wardrobe."

"If you're sure, Netta?" Mother asked the question for form's sake; I could already hear her planning what to pack, deciding whose horses would be best to carry us down the mountain.

"Yes." I wouldn't inflict my crow's voice on my patient family, but I hummed under my breath as I brewed a pot for Uncle. Bark tea, since Skoeran ships hadn't brought us true leaves in ages. Sweetened, it didn't taste too much like dirt.

"You're Mademoiselle Netta? The princess will be so pleased you've come." A small, callused hand took mine, helping me out of the hired carriage and across the drive. Loose gravel rolled under our boots. "I'm Elise, her maid."

"Pleased to meet you, Elise." Mother had stopped to talk with Madame Pevrel, but the strange girl had me securely in tow. I'd greet the housekeeper later.

After the fusty air inside the carriage, the cold breeze slapped my cheeks and pinched my nose, mischievous as a lutin. No snow here; the air wasn't soft enough. I kept wanting to put my hand up to shield my face from the stares I could feel, but perhaps I was imagining the servants' interest. Those who recognized me would make themselves known. I had no enemies here.

"Steps," the maid said. Thoughtful, but not pushy. I liked her already. "Last one."

Double doors opened. The left-side hinges needed oil, I noticed, and then the mingled smells of lemon oil and wood smoke told me I was in the palace's entry hall.

"Welcome back to Lumielle, mademoiselle."

"Thank you..." I searched my memory. The friendly voice belonged to a footman, nose like a turnip. "...Barret," I finished, so triumphantly that we both laughed.

"That's right," Barret said. "You need anything, Elise knows where to find me."

"You're very kind."

The maid escorted me down a long hall. "Princess Aurelie's with the falconer this afternoon. Madame Pevrel said to put you in the chamber next to the Heir's Suite, but I can clear out of the little closet off her sitting room if you'd rather be close to the princess."

"Please, don't move on my account." It brought me up short, though. My status might have changed. Was I a companion or an employee? As a child, I'd slept in my mother's room, in the wing with the upper ranks of servants and artisans. She'd go back there, snug with her cronies, but I hadn't thought further than managing the journey and helping Aurelie when I arrived.

As what? Sighted, I would have followed her anywhere. Blind, I could make lace and tea and mind a baby and map a landscape in my mind—and listen. What if the princess didn't need any of those things?

I would know, I reminded myself. When I heard her voice, I would know what to do. Carpet, stone, carpet again, the soft pile muffling our footsteps. Twenty-two steps from the last turn.

"The Heir's Suite," Elise announced, and we went inside. "I'll see to your unpacking, mademoiselle, and bring some refreshment, if you don't mind waiting here by yourself?"

What a tactful soul, giving me a chance to familiarize myself with these rooms again when no pitying eyes could witness me fumbling around the furniture. "That will suit excellently. Thank you, Elise."

"Back soon, mademoiselle." The latch clicked.

I bashed my shins against a footstool and bruised my hip on the sharp desk edge as I worked my slow way around the sitting room, refurnishing it in my mind. Brocade armchairs, marquetry tables, a daybed draped in velvet. The tiny maid's room offered little more than a bed and dresser, a posy of dried lavender next to the hand mirror and comb. Just in time, I remembered the steps down to the marble bath and crouched to run my fingers along the cool, smooth edge. Aurelie's bedroom hadn't changed. Wardrobe, dressers, two stone maidens holding up the mantelpiece, a flute case on the table beside the immense bed, which was large enough for two little girls and an army of dolls. No dolls today, just a smooth expanse of coverlet and a feather bolster.

I worked my way back to an armchair in the sitting room. I must have slept. The creak of the opening door startled me from a lovely dream in which Loic and I were dancing. My question came out sharper than I intended. "Who's there?"

"Netta!" Princess Aurelie. Glad, her voice, but edged with a darker emotion. Guilt? Worry? Hard to tell from the one word.

"Did you get Mother's letter?"

"Oh, Netta!"

I don't know which of us was more surprised when she hurled herself across the room, put her cold arms around my neck, and burst into tears.

CHAPTER 14

Aurelie

Aurelie's woes poured out of her like milk from a pitcher. Nothing had gone right in Dorisen. Garin pretended not to know her, and never explained why, though they'd met several times. When she'd finally caught him alone, Garin had dumped her in a skiff and gone to warn Elise and Count Sicard. Their departure had started the war all over again. Aurelie had tried so hard to navigate the murky waters of Skoeran politics, but she bungled things so badly! And there was still so much she didn't understand.

Netta's throaty voice murmured comforting noises. She rubbed Aurelie's shoulders.

Aurelie sat up and wiped her nose. "I'm sorry. It's just that I couldn't put any of that in a letter that your mother would read. Everyone acts like I was brave, fighting the fire and escaping from Dorisen, but I was so scared most of the time, and even more now. It'll be bad, Netta."

"How so?"

"The past two years have been mostly insults and skirmishes. We'd confiscate Skoe's ships; they'd fire on ours, maybe raid our coastal farms, or the logging operations on the border with Alsinha."

"What's changed?"

"The Alsinhalese have cut off trade to us and Skoe, both, demanding lower tariffs. The Skoerans are facing a winter with nothing but fish and seaweed broth to eat," Aurelie answered frankly. "Their islands are chunks of rock; they can't grow enough to feed all their people. Skoerans brag about their luxuries, but they can't eat silks and satins. Most of their food comes from abroad. Papa thinks their council will mount an invasion to secure our timber for their ships, our farmland for their larders."

"Mm." Netta's brow puckered. "And what else?"

Aurelie rocked back on her heels. How did her friend know? Was she reading minds, these days? "Isn't that enough?"

"Aurelie," Netta said sternly, "if we have to fight the Skoerans, we'll fight. But I can hear there's something more. You sound exhausted. Something personal, maybe, keeping you up nights. Bad dreams?"

Aurelie couldn't lie to that loving, concerned, blind face. She picked at the rug's fringe. "Personal, yes. Not bad, like the war, rather the opposite. It's Loic."

Netta's breath caught. "You're dreaming about Loic?"

"Not dreaming." In another rush, Aurelie explained how the river drac had surprised her in the carriage. "You made it plain you wanted no more dealings with them, or I'd have contrived to get word to you. He invited me to a revel. A few hours, he promised, with no one the wiser. Oh, Netta." Aurelie let out an awed breath. "I can't describe how beautiful it is. Loic was right. No one noticed. Most nights since, I hear a tap, tap, tapping on the floor, and a door opens, and a crowd of lutins arrives to chivvy me down the stairs into another world, the Fae world. I play my flute and dance with them, and return before dawn."

"That doesn't sound bad," Netta said, when Aurelie ran out of words.

"No, it's wonderful!" Aurelie had heard the wistfulness in her friend's voice. She seized Netta's hands. "You could come, too," she said. "Loic would be glad to invite you!"

Netta tensed. "No, I couldn't. To explain, to have him pity me? I don't want that."

"But it's so delicious," Aurelie coaxed.

"No," Netta said, sharply.

"Think about it, anyway. The moment I'm back in my bed, I'm counting the hours until I can go again and forget all the awful things. Loic doesn't talk about politics."

Netta patted Aurelie's hands and withdrew her own, folding them in her lap. "Then why are you so upset?"

"Why, because it's not real. It's like a play, and then I come home, and nothing's changed. It feels...selfish."

"So you've forgotten your cares for a while," Netta said. "Who would blame you? Many people would find the lost hours a fair trade."

"And some people would consider a night slugging down Captain Inglis's 'private reserve' worth the morning they'd spend puking in a gutter," Aurelie retorted. "I don't happen to be one of them."

"With that sweet girl Elise as a chaperone?" Netta's eyebrows climbed to her hairline. "Your letters didn't mention the part about your drunken binges."

"D-drunken binges?" Aurelie sputtered. "One sip, and that was an accident. I thought it was water."

"If you say so." Netta grinned. "Remember the time you let Loic give your grandmother's goats that fairy wine?"

"He promised me it would make their milk better."

"Better for something," Netta said austerely.

Aurelie giggled, relieved by the change of subject. "It was funny, wasn't it, Madame Brebisse singing to the tin peddler?"

"My luh-luh-love seeks o'er the muh-muh-mountain," Netta warbled.

When Elise pushed the door open with her tray of tea and cakes, she found her mistress flat on the floor, weeping with laughter, while the blind woman wheezed for breath. The maid put the tray on a table, curtsied, and tiptoed away.

Assisted by food and drink of a nonalcoholic nature, Aurelie and Netta regained their composure. The princess ate a seed cake in two bites. "I have missed you, Netta. Most of the courtiers went home to their country estates. The rest are obsessed with war plans. Not that I would mention the Fae to anyone, including Papa."

"Of course you can tell me, and I hope you will," Netta said. "If you go dancing—"

"*When* I go," Aurelie said glumly. "I can't seem to refuse Loic."

"No." Netta sighed. "When you go, then, enjoy it for both of us. You'll tell me about it, and I'll feel I've visited, too. Will that serve?"

"Yes." Aurelie yawned so wide her jaw cracked.

"You're tired." Netta dusted crumbs off her hands. "I'm next door, Elise said."

Aurelie stood and linked arms with her friend, though she noticed that the blind girl moved without hesitation through the sitting room. Aurelie opened the door and pressed her cheek against Netta's. "Good night. Thank you again for coming, and for listening, and for being my friend. I can't remember when I last laughed so hard."

"A long time ago," Netta answered. "For me, too."

Only a passing lutin observed that the blind woman waited until Aurelie's door had closed to feel her way along the wall to the next door and open it. If he had followed her into the chamber, he might have wondered why she stood still for several moments, then seized a bed bolster and mashed it against her face as if she were trying to smother herself.

Or he might not. Everyone knew what odd creatures humans were. They had the lifespan of mayflies, and about as much sense.

Chapter 15

Aurelie

Snug in the Heir's Suite, Aurelie heard nothing out of the ordinary. Later, when the lutins came, she accompanied them with a light heart. She had felt alone for so long, and now two of her dearest friends had been restored to her. If only the third would come, too.... With an almost physical effort, she banished Garin from her mind. He'd made it clear he wanted nothing better than to put a wide stretch of water between them.

It was silly to dwell on rocky Skoe when she stood with both feet planted in the Fae world. Moonlight poured into the dancing glade, polishing the dew-damp moss. Globes of fruit spangled the dark foliage of surrounding trees, and the warm wind played with her unbound hair. Aurelie lifted her face to breathe in its rich scent, sandalwood mixed with bitter orange. For Netta's sake as well as her own, she must store up the night's delight to share in the morning.

Aurelie stretched her arms to the sky, like an evergreen shaking off a load of wet snow. The sudden release of weight made her giddy. "Again," she demanded, turning in the circle of her partner's arms. The playful mood stealing over her was new. Netta's gift, it must be. Aurelie gave silent thanks for her friend's understanding. "Faster, Loic!"

"Faster, little mortal?" Violet-blue eyes widened in amusement.

"Yes." Aurelie bounced on the springy moss. "Unless you're tired?"

"Never," the drac said. "Who falters first pays the other a forfeit?"

"Done!" With a toss of her head, Aurelie accepted the wager. She rested her hand on her escort's arm.

Scales glittered at his wrist. Tonight, the river drac wore a human shape for dancing and with it, a kind of armor. Made of interlocking, flexible plates, the shirt and leggings fitted together so cleverly that they never pinched the folds of her nightgown, no matter how closely he held her. Loic clasped her shoulder; his other arm locked around her waist, and they danced across the clearing. Slowly at first.

Aurelie listened to the wind in the trees, the river whispering secrets to the stars. Later, the Fae would gather to hear her play her flute, but first they danced to the sounds of the elements: earth and air, water and fire. Loud and rolling as thunder or soft as the brush of wings, this world's rhythms were as varied and mysterious as its inhabitants.

When they were younger, the human children had never ventured very close to Loic's home for fear of encountering his parents or mortal nurse. The little drac hadn't minded; he enjoyed exploring the forests and fields of the mortal world. Grown up, Loic proved a gracious host, eager to show off the Fae realm's splendor.

Safe under a full-grown river drac's protection, Aurelie had no fear of a lesser Fae attacking her, like the elder drac had blinded Netta. Still, the early years shadowed them. Most nights Aurelie would catch Loic glancing over his shoulder while they danced, as if he, too, wondered where the others had wandered.

At least she was making a memory to share with Netta. When the dance's tempo quickened, Aurelie met the challenge. Loic twirled her over the moss and then, in a series of gliding steps, guided her out of the clearing and into the forest. It was darker among the trees, but the drac never faltered. He lifted Aurelie in a half turn and tucked her against his chest. She let her head fall against his shoulder, matching his every step. She didn't need to worry about her footing, even when the ground changed to hard-packed dirt and logs covered in drifts of leaves. The strong hand at her waist kept her from stumbling. And if, privately, she wished Loic's skin weren't quite so *scaly*, she didn't say so.

They leaped and dipped and spun through a narrow ravine, where the night's song echoed in Aurelie's ears, and then out of the sheltering forest to the riverbank. Bordered with trailing water weeds, the current polished diamond-bright grains of sand. Loic spun Aurelie to face him, and they swooped in wide circles beside the river. Aurelie's hair swung away from her face. Her nightgown belled out from her body; she thought they might be flying.

And then a turn swept her feet into the water. The shock felt delicious against her ankles, but surprise was her undoing. She gasped.

Losing her footing, she sank in a breathless heap on the ground. "That was a low trick." She scooped up a handful of water and flicked it at Loic.

Untroubled by the droplets running down his armor, the drac lounged beside her, his legs outstretched. "Did I lag behind you?"

"No," Aurelie admitted.

"Then I claim my forfeit."

Aurelie glanced at him from under her eyelashes. "I don't recall agreeing to the stakes," she demurred.

"No, sweet mortal?" Loic tugged on a lock of her hair. "Then I must accept whatever reward you care to bestow."

Aurelie leaned over and propped her elbows on his chest. The flexible plates of armor shimmered. She ran her hand over the unusual garment. Not metal or leather or cloth. It was cool, and smelled...she put her nose closer and sniffed. It smelled like breakfast in a spring meadow: wild strawberries and grilled mushrooms and oatcakes with butter. She thumped his chest. "What is this?"

The violet eyes blinked lazily. "What of my forfeit?"

"Mm." Distracted, Aurelie stared into Loic's handsome face. "Your forfeit?" she repeated. "Let me think."

"As you will." His mouth curved at the corners.

How would the others respond? Garin hated to lose. He'd suggest another contest, best of three. And Netta? Aurelie leaned closer, her lips a breath away. "A kiss," she said.

"Acceptable," Loic replied.

The Fae tasted the way his strange armor smelled, tart and wild and a little earthy. River reeds, and musk. Delicious. Dangerous.

Aurelie drew back, aware of unease sliding down her spine. Perhaps that hadn't been such a good idea.

A voice snapped in her ear. "Bad princess!"

The world reversed itself. Or rather, *she* did, Aurelie understood after a confused moment. Loic had dropped her, putting himself between Aurelie and a newcomer. More than one, she corrected herself, peering over Loic's shoulder. Other Fae had found them.

Her escort did not sound pleased. "Helis."

"Kiss, kiss." The fox-faced lutine smacked her lips and peered at them through locks of russet hair. She brandished Aurelie's wooden flute. "Enough kisses. Play!"

"Let me catch my breath, Helis." Blushing, Aurelie took the flute and stood to shake the creases out of her nightgown. Loic stepped aside so Aurelie could greet the other two Fae. "Good evening, Yvaire, Gaelle."

Another lutine, Yvaire's lapis-colored eyes shone behind a birdlike mask of iridescent plumage. Blue and purple feathers tickled Aurelie's wrist as the Fae dipped her head. She didn't speak, but Aurelie wasn't insulted. Yvaire never did.

The tall Fée Verte folded Aurelie in her arms. "We missed you, Princess," Gaelle said. Her mantle of whispering leaves surrounded Aurelie. It felt like being embraced by a tree that wore a wood nymph's face. Noisy and ticklish.

"We were dancing," Aurelie said, as Gaelle stepped back to nod her leaf-crowned head at Loic.

"Dancing?" Helis made a rude noise.

Loic ignored the red-haired lutine. He bowed to Gaelle, then offered Yvaire one arm and Aurelie the other. Helis darted ahead and disappeared among the trees as the drac escorted the others back to the clearing where the dance had begun. "Until soon, my lovelies," he said, his voice at its most resonant.

Aurelie felt honored to be included with the others. "Until soon." She curtsied, watching him stride away, then settled herself on the moss.

Gaelle had followed at a slower pace, stopping to pick a pear-shaped fruit from an overhanging branch. "Will you take Loic for your lover?" the Fée Verte asked idly.

"Oh, no." Aurelie touched her tongue to her lips. "We're just, ah, friends." Netta might have had a different answer, but then she should have come herself. To cover her embarrassment, Aurelie found her flute case and took out a polishing cloth. She pulled the instrument apart and wiped each section clean.

Gaelle's gown rustled as she sat, spreading the scent of cedar bark. The Fae's twiggy fingers measured the fruit she had picked. With a deft twist, the Fae divided it in two and offered half to Aurelie.

Aurelie accepted with a nod of thanks, admiring the fruit's rosy skin. At the first taste, her eyes closed, the better to savor it. The flesh burned on her tongue, then dissolved in a rush of sweetness, as if she had eaten fire dipped in honey. Garin would love these. The Fae had bolder tastes even than Skoerans. Food here was hotter, sharper, sweeter, more intense—like their dancing, their conversation, their kisses.

Aurelie shivered and opened her eyes, then stared at her empty hand. She had taken one bite. Where had the rest of the fruit gone?

"Helis." Gaelle's tone made the name a warning.

Aurelie turned around in puzzlement. Behind her, the russet-haired lutine licked her snout. "Helis!" Aurelie said. "Give it back."

"Gone." Fox ears twitched. Two sticky fingers tapped the flute case. "Play."

"I said I would, before you stole my treat." Aurelie made a face at the lutine.

Helis sniffed. "You promised."

Aurelie relented. "So I did." In honor of the approaching season, she played the winter round that children sang on the Longest Night. The notes dropped crisp and clear from her flute, telling of distant stars, snow on the wind, the hush that falls over the world before the season changes.

She looked up once from her fingering to see Loic's violet eyes fixed intently on hers. As if the Fae's gaze had summoned it, a wisp of memory drifted through Aurelie's mind. The same song but a different setting. She let the notes remind her.

Warm. Toasty warm, though cold air bit her little nose when she poked it out of the nest of furs. *Dark.* A winter's night, with lines of torches that pierced the darkness and dropped ash onto the snow. Bells tinkled. A horse snorted. Beneath the moon, the sleigh glided, iron runners squeaking on packed snow.

Content, and safe, and sleepy. Aurelie marveled at how distinctly she remembered. She must have been very small; the figures on either side of her loomed large on the sleigh bench. One sang, his deep voice opening the round. Aurelie loved to hear her papa sing. She snuggled next to him, waiting for the moment her mama would chime in—there! The sweet, breathy voice chased the low, steady voice, like a puppy chasing its tail. Around and around.

Aurelie's eyelids fluttered as she played the simple tune, fingers moving up and down the flute. Around and around. She was child Aurelie, drifting into sleep...she was grown Aurelie, playing for the Fae. *Safe, beloved.* The moon shone overhead. Aurelie's eyes opened and locked onto Loic's fathomless gaze. What big eyes the river drac had. Aurelie was falling. As if the memory were a dark lake, she dropped into it and saw a woman with chestnut hair and dark eyes. Her bronze skin glowed in the torchlight as Queen Basia tucked a lap robe around her daughter. "Sweet dreams, Aurelie."

The tenderness of the gesture tightened Aurelie's throat. "Mama," she whispered into the flute, and brought the song to a close. A swift, sharp pain stabbed her chest. She would never see that face again, never hear the soft voice call her name. Aurelie couldn't breathe; she couldn't move. Loic's deep eyes held hers, and for a moment she was frightened by the hunger she read there. Then the Fae blinked, releasing her, and Aurelie knew again who she was and where and why. She was safe with the Fae, of course she was safe. What had prompted that moment of unease? She had felt trapped, almost, by the drac's regard.

She couldn't quite...what had she...? Aurelie reached for an answer, but it was gone, and unimportant, after all, when lutins and farfadets crowded around her knees, crowing with pleasure. She reflected how odd it was, to have left her home and everything familiar behind, only to discover her family waiting here. True, Queen Basia had died. But when Aurelie played, her mother's memory lived, immortal as the Fae.

Had his own memories drawn Loic back to the mortal world? Perhaps, in all the splendor of the Fae realm, he'd never found companionship sweeter than what he'd shared with his human friends?

Gaelle plaited Aurelie's hair with her twiggy fingers. Loic smiled his lazy smile and stroked the arch of Aurelie's bare foot. "Acceptable, dearest Princess," he teased.

"Another!" Helis said.

Aurelie played a second song, and then a third. Music was the one gift she could offer in return for the magical time Loic's favor had opened to her, and she gave it gladly.

When the hour came for Aurelie to depart, the drac escorted Aurelie to her bedchamber. He kissed the back of her hand, his lips lingering, then took his leave. As she pulled the bedclothes over her head, Aurelie sighed in exhausted contentment. She couldn't wait to tell Netta.

CHAPTER 16

Garin

I hid in the library. An old building, it had been added onto many times, with walls knocked out between adjacent properties, stairs and ramps added to connect the levels. Two nights running, I managed to keep out of sight, taking catnaps in areas the cleaners had swept and dusted the previous day. Most of the time, though, I read, trying to find something in the archives that would help me clear my name.

A lutine had given me the idea, the night Burgida had told me about the order for my arrest. I'd escaped just ahead of the guards and fallen asleep beneath an overturned dinghy. When I awoke, my hair had been twisted into tiny plaits tied with feathers and limpet shells. Together with a scruff of beard and the patched black scholar's gown I'd picked up in a shop behind the university, I hoped to pass for a foreign student. People traveled here from great distances to read history, geography, philosophy, medicine. The gown helped me blend in with the library's other patrons and was too shabby, I hoped, to catch the eyes of Inglis's toughs on the street. But the capital wasn't large. I didn't have much time before my pursuers widened their search beyond the docks.

And my prospects looked grim. Several weeks after Princess Aurelie's ship left for Lumielle, Captain Inglis had accused me of setting the fire and offered a reward for my capture. I wondered whether she had recognized me when she hired me for *Gargouille*'s crew, or whether she learned my identity later and adjusted her plans. In any case, her story contained just enough truth to be plausible: a rival merchant's son spying on her affairs. Her bribes made the fiction reality, at least to the council's satisfaction. While blaming me, she'd been careful not to include my parents. Their allies wouldn't support a total condemnation of my family or the confiscation of their remaining property.

No, I was the goat. My parents had to distance themselves, and I encouraged them to do so, the one time I'd sneaked into the loft above the repair yard. Rigger Neff had been Inglis's watcher that night. Finding a bottle of brandy in the alley had kept him distracted, but even he would suspect a trick if it happened a second time.

Although my family knew the truth, there was no telling what the princess had heard. Had she made it safely home? Surely, or the news would have penetrated even the library's quiet corridors. Would Aurelie believe the lies Inglis had spread about me?

I hoped not, though I couldn't have inspired much confidence the last time she saw me: filthy, curt to the point of rudeness, stomping away quick as I could to hide how much I wanted to stay. When she flew out of the box-chair, so pretty and sweet-smelling, it was like she belonged to another world. I couldn't put her down fast enough to stop my sooty clothes from staining her dress. And then, like a fool, I'd accused her people of starting the fire. Hadn't I felt the bandages on her hands, under the lace, the same as my own mother and every other Dorisen citizen?

Aurelie had trusted me, picking my box-chair from the line. She'd hurt her hands fighting for my city. I hadn't even thanked her, just shoved her into the skiff and left, convincing myself it was thoughtfulness, not hurt pride, that kept me from sharing my problems. I meant to help, keeping her out of Inglis's clutches. Except that my meddling had exploded in our faces, and set the captain harder against the Jocondagnans for the insult to her house.

Why didn't Inglis want peace between our countries? If I knew more, perhaps I could counter her moves, not just run while her men chased me around the board. She needed to bring me in soon. Preferably dead, I assumed, so I'd be unable to plead my own case or ask questions about the fire. Like how I'd set it while cooking supper for the Woolies.

Neff had wondered, I'd heard, but been shut up by a technical explanation of fuses and lead times. Which meant anyone could have done the deed. Who stood to gain? Inglis.

But I had to prove it. The cryptic notes in her little ledger had given me ideas, but nothing solid. I would have to find a thread of inconsistency elsewhere and tug at it until the cloth of her lies came unraveled. I started with the Fae.

Dorisen's library possessed a large number of books on the

subject, considering that only lutins and the occasional silkie or mermaid visited Skoe. When the greater Fae entered the mortal world, they shunned our rocky isles.

On second thought, perhaps it was safer to study the creatures from a distance. They might not tolerate having their secrets published too close to their haunts. While Jocondagnans told stories, I'd never seen a book about the Fae on the continent, even in the king's palace in Lumielle.

Keeping an ear to the door, and both feet on the floor, I skimmed the brittle pages. Most of it was nonsense, third- and fourth-hand tales written by people who'd never met the Fae and so gave an exaggerated picture of their powers. Contrary to several reports, suck-breaths couldn't kill a person. As a child in Cantrez, I'd forgotten to put a piece of bread under my pillow one summer night and woken from a bad dream to find one of the ugly things crouched on my chest. My sitting up and shouting had frightened her. Like rats, they fed off the helpless, skittering away the moment a person opened his eyes.

When I found a description of a gargouille, supposedly copied from the journal of a man who'd courted her human shape (and survived), I hoped it was a similar exaggeration. A dragon the size of a whale, magic-working, fire-breathing, *hungry*, without a river drac's sense of humor or a Fée Verte's love of dancing to recommend her? The last one had been sighted near Lumielle a hundred years ago. For my friends' sake, I hoped she never chose to return to her lair under the River Sicaun.

Loic had told us that the Fae generally preferred their world. They visited ours from time to time as a wealthy Dorisen merchant might spend an evening at a dockyard dive, to remind himself why he liked the heights.

Matagots, lutins, White Ladies, melusines…Madame Brebisse had spoken about many of them. I kept myself alert by grading the authors' claims. *River dracs employ human nurses to care for their young.* True. *Once lured into the river, the nurse is bound for seven years.* True. *Her service ends when the young drac kills and eats her.* False. Loic said dracs enjoyed our conversation, not our flesh. When her term ended, a nurse was returned to her astonished family with a purse of gold and a warning that she must never speak of her employers. As a foster child myself, I had wondered what happened to the nurse's own children in the meantime. The stories didn't address the question.

Out of respect for the librarians, I didn't write on the books, however much I was tempted. Page followed page, a mix of solid information, half truths, and lies, until at last I found a picture that resembled Helm Burgida's Fae form.

Holding the book to the light, I struggled to decipher the old-fashioned text.

The Vouivre wears her Luck like a Living Gem. To Bathe, she puts the Jewel aside for Safe Keeping and assumes the Face and Form of a beautiful Woman. At this Moment, a Bold and Enterprising Person may Attempt its Acquisition and Enjoy Seven Years of Excellent Fortune, though Few succeed in the Attempt. Deadly when Roused, the Vouivre's Talons and Teeth will Rend her unfortunate Victim to Pieces.

I studied the picture again. Lizard body, long snout, two big eyes, and set in her forehead, an enormous, glittering gem. Not so for the Fae I'd seen. Either the author was mistaken about it, or someone had stolen Helm Burgida's Luck.

Captain Inglis? Was that how she compelled a Fae to be her servant? What other powers did the stone confer? And what happened when the seven years were up?

At the beat of approaching footsteps, I closed the book and spread an ocean atlas over it. Good thing, too. As if my thoughts had summoned her, Burgida entered the room.

She slid into the seat opposite me, stretched out her legs, and nodded at the atlas. "Planning a trip?"

"Maybe." The empty hollow in her forehead drew my eye. I looked at the atlas. Why had Burgida helped me escape? Did it amuse her to thwart Inglis in this small thing, given the circumstances?

"I'm no physician," the Fae said, "but I believe a change of scene would be good for your health."

"A southern climate, perhaps?"

Her boot pushed a leather knapsack across the floor. It bumped my leg with the soft clank of coin. "Certain parties are investing in extra 'protection.' Cold, cold weather on the way, they say."

Perhaps she, too, wanted to escape. "And you? Fancy a sea voyage?"

"No, thanks." She smiled. My doubled vision showed me a forked tongue, flickering between a muzzle full of sharp teeth. "I've a contract to fulfill."

"Then I owe you."

"You do, aye." Another toothy smile, under the sad eyes. "Why else would I keep quiet and spot you the gear?"

"About that…" I let the words hang, an invitation.

She didn't care to explain herself. "Fair winds," she said, and strolled out of the library, boot heels clicking on the stone.

Burgida had found me, in itself a warning. Others couldn't be far behind. Paying a boy to deliver a note to my parents, I boarded an outbound vessel that same afternoon.

CHAPTER 17

Aurelie

"Outside, Your Highness? At this hour?" The footman turned from Aurelie to Netta as if he hoped for a more sensible answer from the blind girl, although she, too, wore a coat, hat, and gloves. "In this weather?"

"A little fresh air before bed," Netta said. "We're only going as far as the garden, Barret."

The footman's face turned pink at the recognition. "Yes, mademoiselle. Your Highness."

He opened the door, and frigid night air rushed in. Before Aurelie could take Netta's elbow, her friend strode down the steps and turned left at the bottom. "The Long Walk or the maze?"

"Maze," Aurelie said. Side by side, they walked down the flagstone path. Their breath made twin clouds of vapor, and their boots crunched the dried leaves that skittered along, pushed by the wind.

As they reached the tall hedge around the maze, footsteps pounded behind them. Aurelie hailed the running footman. "What is it, Barret?"

"Mortal cold out, Your Highness," he said, looking at Netta. "Borrowed a pair of sentry capes for you and mademoiselle."

"How thoughtful of you," Aurelie said.

The footman draped the heavy bearskin capes over their shoulders. A square of golden light from the palace windows above them showed his concerned face. "You'll be wanting a lantern, ladies?"

"No, thank you." Mischief warmed Netta's voice. "Day or night, I promise not to lose the princess in the maze. Without the light, she'll have a better view of the stars."

"Yes, mademoiselle." Barret bowed.

"Shall we?" Netta offered her arm, and Aurelie accepted.

As they entered the maze, the leafless hedges blocked some of the wind's force. Netta sniffed. "What do you smell?" Aurelie asked.

"Oh." Netta laughed a bit self-consciously and pulled the cape's hood over her head. "The weather. Snow coming, I think. Tomorrow night, maybe sooner."

Aurelie sniffed, too. "All I smell is gunpowder from the cannons they've been firing at the practice range." The taste of it caught in her throat, reminding her of Dorisen and the fire. "The eagles didn't like it. Only Paumera and Montbrai would come to the glove today, and I can't blame them. The noise gave me a headache."

"I meant to ask you about the training," Netta said. "You seemed distracted before supper."

"Mm." Aurelie paused. "Left here or right?"

"Whatever you like."

Aurelie turned left, then left again. She trailed her gloved hand across the wall of bare twigs. The leafless hedges seemed ghostly in the starlight, as if, with a little imagination, a person could part them like smoke and walk into another world. The Fae realm, perhaps. "You can really keep all our changes of direction in your head?"

Netta chuckled. "Now you're asking?"

"I suppose the footman would wonder what had happened to us."

"If you don't get around to saying what's bothering you, Barret will no doubt come to our rescue," Netta said. "The capes will only buy us so much time."

Aurelie blew out a puff of breath. "You're right, of course. It's an awkward subject. I didn't want Elise or the housekeeper or your mother interrupting."

"I gathered that. And I have news for you, too. Go ahead, you first."

"I feel so silly, but there's no one else I can ask, and I have to tell someone," Aurelie blurted out. "Is there any reason...have you heard of the Fae and a mortal...is Loic *courting* me?"

"What?" Netta stopped, pulling Aurelie off-balance.

"I know, I know." Aurelie fanned her burning cheeks. "It sounds so odd. Conceited, almost, to think such a thing."

Netta dropped Aurelie's arm and retreated into her cape, like a turtle into its shell. "Why do you ask?"

"The kissing," Aurelie said. As a muffled squeak emerged from Netta's hood, Aurelie bit her lip. "I didn't want to distress you, Netta, so I haven't mentioned it, but…It's warmer, walking. You don't mind, do you?" She peered at her friend, but darkness and bearskin hid Netta's expression.

"No, you'd better tell me." Netta marched forward, and Aurelie skipped after her, relieved to get this out in the open.

"So, the first couple of times it was lovely, melty and delicious…anyway, I liked it very much. Not proper, you're right. I told myself I should put a stop to it. But Loic, *you* know, those irresistible violet eyes…and he's grown up, like we have, so it wasn't like kissing the little drac who cut up his nurse's aprons for pirate flags and put spiders down our backs."

Netta nodded.

"It's just that, lately, he's acting so peculiar! He doesn't want me dancing with farfadets or lutins, only him. He keeps suggesting I might like to see other parts of the Fae world. The other night, I thought for a moment that he might not take me home when I asked. As if I would abandon Jocondagne, and Father, with everyone on the brink of war!"

"The kissing?" Netta prompted, when Aurelie fell silent.

"Yes. Well, it's nice, but I feel like he's kissing an idea of me. As if, when our lips meet, he's closing his eyes because if he really looked at me, he'd be disappointed. I wouldn't measure up to this image he's created of a marriageable mortal woman." Aurelie scrubbed her gloved hands together. "How ridiculous I sound. Forget it. Forget I said anything."

"Loic couldn't be disappointed in you, Aurelie," Netta said evenly. "You're a princess through and through."

"A princess?" Aurelie scoffed. "Worse than that, I'm the Heir. Can you imagine a Fae like Loic taking responsibility for a boring mortal kingdom? No, he's not after my title and hardly my wealth. The Door to the Fae world is inside a cave with treasure stacked higher than my head, but he never gives it a second glance."

"Do you"—Netta cleared her throat—"do you care for him?"

"Of course. But of the two of us, I always thought Loic preferred you. That's another reason I had to say something. You won't come with me, and you won't let me tell him you're here. Meanwhile, he keeps kissing me. It makes me sick, lying to both of you."

"What about Garin?"

Aurelie was glad of the dark and her own hood. "I don't see how he figures in." Her voice shook a little, but she steadied it. "He had lots of chances to talk to me in Dorisen, but every time I saw him, he was too busy doing something more important."

"Like helping you get away from the Inglises?" Netta said.

"The last time, yes. But he never once said he was glad to see me or that he'd missed me or that he wanted to be friends again."

"And you mentioned all those things to him?"

"Netta!" Aurelie put her hands on her hips. "Whose side are you on?"

"Yours, Your Highness. Always," Netta said, so stiffly that Aurelie hugged her.

"Please don't be angry. You're right, I could have spoken first. Garin and I've both got more pride than good sense, I'm afraid."

"Not the only one," Aurelie thought she heard, but when asked to repeat it, Netta shook her head.

"My feet are freezing. I won't last out here much longer. It may not signify, but my news has to do with Garin, too."

"He's not hurt?" Aurelie's face felt numb, her lips two chips of ice. "You wouldn't have kept that from me?"

"No, no. It's about the fire. Mother's friends were gossiping in her workroom today. Someone's cousin had traded for a load of smuggled cloth and got news along with the goods. Dorisen's council ruled the fire was set on purpose. Not by Jocondagnans, though. Garin's been accused of the crime."

Outrage melted some of the frost that had chilled Aurelie to the bone. "Burning his own family's ships and warehouse? That's absurd."

"Captain Inglis claims it was a revenge gone wrong. He'd been working for her under a false name. Supposedly, he only meant to burn her goods, not knowing that his family was responsible for everything stored in their warehouse. Then the fire got out of control."

Aurelie remembered Garin dressed in *Gargouille*'s gold and crimson, his evasiveness at the iceboat warehouse, his asking whether her people had set the fire. He hadn't told her everything, but she couldn't believe him a villain. "He must have had a good reason for whatever he was doing. Inglis is lying."

"Of course she is. This way." Netta pulled Aurelie to the right. "Garin disappeared before they could put him in prison, and Inglis has offered a reward for his capture. It's big, enough to buy a small farm or a racehorse."

"What do we do?" Dread, more than cold, made Aurelie shiver. "How can we help him?"

"I've been thinking. First, we make sure that the report is true. About what the council determined, I mean. We know Garin is innocent."

"And then?"

Netta shrugged. "And then we wait. Where would *you* go, if Lumielle turned against you?"

"To Cantrez, to Grand-mère's farm. Or wherever you were, Netta."

"And if we couldn't help you?"

"G-garin," Aurelie said, tentatively, and then with more confidence, "or Loic. He pretends to be above mortal concerns, but he cares more than he lets on. Maybe more than he realizes. Of course, I'd have to find him first. When he's in a disappearing mood…" She spread her hands wide.

"About Loic." Netta's steps slowed, as if she sensed the yellow squares of light shining from the palace.

They'd reached the maze's final corridor. Clever Netta, walking, talking, and navigating, while Aurelie could barely put one leaden foot in front of the other. Hearing of Garin's danger had thrown her feelings in sharp relief, like the lantern casting a long shadow along the pavement outside the maze.

It was the shadow of a footman. Barret, if she wasn't mistaken, venturing into the garden to find them. Aurelie held Netta's elbow, keeping just inside the hedge. Her friend was entitled to her opinion about fools and pride, but would she recognize her own error?

"What about Loic?" Aurelie whispered. "Will you come with me tonight, tell me I'm imagining things?"

"No, I—just don't hurt him, Your Highness," Netta said from the depths of her hood. "Don't lead him on, if you don't truly love him."

Aurelie wanted to shake her, but the footman had seen them. "Your Highness. Mademoiselle," he called, relief plain in his voice.

"Here, Barret," Aurelie said. She and Netta left the maze and walked toward the footman.

"And the stars, Your Highness?" He glanced up at the sky. "Did you enjoy the vista?"

"Oh, yes. Delightful," she lied. Again.

CHAPTER 18

Loic

Because flying dogs attract attention of precisely the wrong sort, I take the shape of a sea eagle for my next survey of the princess's city. It's not an appealing vista. At this season, one might reasonably expect rooftops and avenues draped in elegant white. Instead, a spell of cold, dry weather has settled over the land. Bereft of winter's snowy mantle, Lumielle resembles a slattern too lazy to wash. Soot streaks the slate roofs and stone buildings; silent fountains preside over dirty streets. Clutching the city's two islands to its icy breast, the river has frozen along its length as far as the western sea. Beyond the city walls, the countryside lies brown and bleak. Mud on mud. Ugly. Detestable.

Soaring over Lumielle, this judgment strikes me as a trifle harsh. I am restless this afternoon, which is not uncommon, and spoiling, as men do, for a fight. Which is rather unusual. I pride myself on a benevolent detachment, cultivated at some cost. Unlike mortals, whose young "grow up" by abandoning the evidence of their senses to conform to their elders' prejudices, dracs mature in strength and wisdom. Ever more keenly, we recognize the folly that informs our mutual existence, and delight in sharing that knowledge with the deluded creatures. What have humans, with their limited faculties, to teach a drac?

Only consider how I embarked on my wooing of Princess Aurelie. Each flattering word and tender glance led her inescapably to that first kiss, which the dear soul thought was her idea. So credulous, mortals. I enjoyed it, too. Pretty girls, Fées Vertes, the occasional lutine (though not that vulgar Helis)…many have called me an excellent lover. Darling Aurelie will, too.

All proceeds as I intend, so I do not understand the tight sensation along my jaw when she speaks, the desire to snap at her—with teeth—for being the girl she is and not another. What's to choose, between mortals? Brown eyes, brown hair, pleasant manners both, the princess perhaps a trifle prone to flights of valor. The other more sensitive, her speaking voice pleasingly husky, her mind lively. Dear Aurelie is a perfectly decent specimen, and she'll make a delightful wife.

She's not *Netta*.

That is the crux of the problem. I'd prefer my humans interchangeable. Time has not sanded fine their particularity, as I had expected. Instead, they've lodged under my skin, these girls; they prickle like burrs. It's as though nothing has changed since we frolicked together, two against two. As if to mock me, the wind carries an echo of distant laughter, a trace of familiar scent. Shall I make myself ridiculous, peering in each windowpane, hoping for a glimpse of one mortal woman's face? Shall I insult Aurelie by asking her to please deliver her replacement?

Not poetic, a sea eagle's scream, but effective.

Far below me, small figures peer skyward. Some hide in doorways, others under trees. In full, glorious voice, I fold my wings and drop from a great height. Horses plunge down the streets; dogs bark. Marching in an open field, a company of raw recruits abandons their weapons and, in some cases, their boots. A timid woman faints against her escort's arm. Faster, faster, a streak of white light with Death's own voice, I swoop toward the river.

More like a phoenix than an eagle, I rise again in majesty. Though the wind blows wet, promising snow, its sluggish breath lifts me. I glide, inhabiting this new shape with my usual ease. Onward I fly from the human city and its conundrums. Busy, busy, busy, the men below fill bags of earth and stack them against the city walls. I leave them to it, following the finger of ice to the marsh at the river's mouth. Just beyond, the ocean surges against a breakwater sheltering several large ships at anchor.

Keen vision, sea eagles. I spy fish swimming in the gray sea. A girl crouches on a ship's deck, polishing brass rails with a rag and powder. Along the shore, men dig trenches in the sand, more fortifications for this war they're all so keen on. Deep in the marsh, a man conceals a small boat under a pile of reeds. Furtive, he peers around (but not up, naturally), then shoulders a knapsack and trudges in the direction of the city.

Oh, ho! Shall I help or hinder him? I follow, contemplating which course of action would provide me with the most entertainment.

When at last he climbs up the stairs from the river landing, I've decided on the shape of our encounter. This section of the bridge connects the royal palace with the southern half of the city. In the center of the span, a high tower rises to defend the island from the water side. Along the bridge's length, the mad and the destitute huddle against the stone railing. Despite the cold, the bridge teems with holidaymakers. Both the begging and the gaiety strike my ear with a desperate note.

I've assumed the form of an old woman, and I am sitting against the statue of a bronze warrior queen atop a prancing horse. Like the other beggars, I've set a ragged cap before me. Unlike them, I do not importune the passing multitudes. As my chosen victim approaches, I push myself up and stagger as if my legs have stiffened on the cold pavement. The horse rearing on its plinth is poised to kick me in the ear, but the man takes my arm and guides me to safety at the railing.

"Steady now, little mother," he says. "Madame's steed has a fiery eye."

"Thank you," I reply in a croaking voice unlike my usual dulcet tones. In a nearsighted fashion, I aim my spectacles at my benefactor. His barber is a lutin, apparently. Twists of brown hair and a scrim of stubble obscure a face older and harder than I remember. The gray-green eyes haven't changed: steady, intelligent, reserved.

Garin picks up the cap and shakes it. "Slow morning, eh?" For the first time, he looks me full in the face. His breath hitches, and those perceptive eyes narrow. Folding the cap over the coins, he tucks it into my gloved hand. "Snow coming before dark. Best save this for later."

"You wouldn't have a bite to share with a hungry soul?" I wheedle.

"All right." He shrugs out of his pack and leans against the bridge railing next to me. A cloth-wrapped bundle yields several smoked fish and a wedge of dry cheese. He divides the food and pushes the larger share toward me. As he should. He's not forgotten, in barren Skoe, how to deal with my kind.

We chew, watching the humans hurry past us: soldiers, students, travelers, all oblivious to the river drac and the Skoeran enjoying a companionable meal in their midst. Street vendors push rattling carts. Children trail after them, pursuing the aromas of hot fruit tarts, spicy soups, roasted chestnuts. I would enjoy a sausage but am too polite to complain at the lack.

Garin stows the empty napkin. "Finished?"

"Yes, thank you."

He tips an imaginary cap before hoisting his pack. "A privilege to dine with such a lovely lady."

Hah! The first sarcasm he's permitted himself. In an instant, we're back on our old footing of friendly rivalry. Garin won't watch me with a troubled frown when he thinks my attention is elsewhere. He won't mince words, trying to spare my supposed feelings when I ask him a simple question. I have no desire to kiss him, and am not troubled by my disinterest. It's enormously refreshing. I block his path. "Where are you going?"

He folds his arms across his chest. "Why, to seek my fortune, madame. Have you a suggestion for me?"

"Absolutely, young sir."

Laugh lines crinkle around his eyes. "Do tell."

"Why not enlist? The army pays decent marksmen a bonus."

The amusement leaves his face. "No soldiering. My heart isn't in the fight, and I don't think this lot would have me."

He jerks his thumb toward the palace, and I remember that, technically, he's Aurelie's enemy. How piquant! Could he be spying on his old playfellow? The hidden boat does suggest a clandestine entry. "A peacemaker, eh? That limits your prospects in Lumielle, young sir."

"Perhaps we could discuss my employment somewhere else?" He casts an uneasy glance up and down the crowded bridge. "A person of your wisdom and experience, madame, might resolve a few questions for me."

In character, I cackle. "Disappointed in love, are we?"

He shifts under the pack and glowers at his boots. "Not that kind of trouble."

"But it's my specialty! Why, just last evening, I entertained the dearest girl. I'm sure you'd enjoy seeing her, too."

Garin's sullen expression dissolves into a fond smile. "So Netta finally came to Lumielle? I thought she hadn't left Cantrez since the—for a couple of years, now."

"Not her. The other one."

"What?"

On another occasion, I'd savor his astonishment. It's not easy to put Garin out of countenance. But I've smelled a lie—no, not so strong: an evasion. Why would he attempt to mislead his old friend the drac? That incident with the goat dung was so long ago; surely the boy wouldn't have been holding it against me all this while.

Indignation swells too large for an old woman's genteel frame to contain. "Netta never left Cantrez?" I forget my persona, and my voice rolls out, too commanding for verisimilitude. A passing goodwife lets out a startled gasp and hurries on.

"We haven't exactly corresponded, with the war, and all," Garin says. Another half truth. His skin exudes unease, sour as old sweat.

"By all means, young man, let us chat in private." I grasp his shoulder. He feels the claws inside the tattered gloves and accompanies me docilely enough down the steps to the river. We make our way along the frozen bank and into a half-ruined building. A door in the far wall opens to my touch. Garin stumbles in the chill darkness, but I'm in no mood to accommodate his deficient vision. Paving gives way to crumbling stairs, another door, this one solid oak, and a rough, unlit passageway that reeks of old stone and older gargouille. I shed the crone form and resume my own shape.

"I assumed the three of you had been called away to the capital, without time for making a proper farewell," I say. "If Netta remained in Cantrez, why did she never visit?"

"You'll have to ask her."

Garin's loyalty is commendable, but inconvenient. My roar thunders in the cavern. "I'm asking YOU."

He is, alas, unimpressed. "Ask the princess, if you're so chummy."

I sense a sore spot and poke at it. "More than chummy. I intend to claim her hand."

"You and Aurelie? Married?" His voice cracks, and then he laughs. The long, relieved sound pursues the fading echoes of my anger. "Oh, very funny, Loic. You've gotten subtler. I fell for it, I admit. Why's she really coming down here?"

"You don't believe me?" My head spins, in a figurative sense. I've been lured into a web of sticky human lies and must fight my way clear, strand by clutching strand. Beginning with the most salient fact I do not yet possess. "Did something happen to my Netta?"

"She's safe," Garin says.

"How do you know?"

"Aurelie told me in Dorisen."

Truth, but not all of it. Maddening that Garin won't satisfy my reasonable inquiries. I'm concerned for a friend's welfare, and what's my reward? Defiance. A stone, or one of Aurelie's grandmother's blockheaded bleaters, would be more forthcoming. "You'll stay with me until we resolve this with the princess."

"Fine." He sounds impatient. "Try her. When Aurelie clams up, which she will, I'd suggest finding Netta and asking her yourself why she stayed away."

Easy for the mortal to say. Dracs in the prime of their power don't crawl to human girls, crying because they've lost favor. But I will know. The princess will tell me, or Garin. Neither will be permitted to leave tonight's revel until I have assured myself of Netta's well-being.

CHAPTER 19

Aurelie

The dying fire muttered and smoked. Aurelie lay in her bed, staring up at the lively scenes painted on the ceiling. Nymphs cavorted, dragons roared, unicorns flaunted their ivory horns. Her head ached; she had woken from a sound sleep to worry about Garin. Netta assured her he would come, but what if Inglis's men had captured him? Or, almost worse, what if he were free but no longer trusted Aurelie enough to make his way to Lumielle? What if he got caught somewhere between the invading Skoeran ships and Jocondagnan defenders? She could imagine a hundred dreadful scenarios, and few hopeful ones.

She couldn't help feeling she'd failed Netta, too. Once again, her friend had refused to accompany Aurelie to the Fae world. Two years it had taken the blind girl to brave the capital. Would the Fae linger near Lumielle while Netta gathered the courage to visit? She obviously longed to do so. Her voice betrayed her whenever she spoke of Loic. Which wasn't so frequently, after the conversation in the maze.

Aurelie thumped her pillow. A tiny noise, soft as the snowflakes brushing her window, caught her attention. She sat up. There it was again! At last, the hour had come. She knew now that she never should have encouraged Loic. If their situations had been reversed and she'd seen the other two kissing, Aurelie would have found it difficult to endure. Why had it taken a threat to Garin to make her understand whose embraces she really wished for?

Tonight she would be kind, but firm. Even if it meant a halt to her visits, she must tell Loic to stop kissing her. For all her friends' sake, this had to stop.

Tap, tap, rattle-tap.

Aurelie knelt by the fireplace and rapped on the floor in answer. *Tap, tap.* The square of flooring by her knees wavered, thinned, and became transparent. In a rush of laughter, several Fae whirled up through the opening.

"Well met, Princess." As each entered, she touched Aurelie's face lightly in greeting. Gauzy robes fluttered like giant moth wings as the Fae flitted around her. In their wake, the boundary between worlds blurred, transforming her chamber. The fire writhed in passionate flames that intensified the rich colors of draperies and walls and painted ceiling. The fragrance of white narcissus spilled from the bowl on the table, adding its sweetness to the mixture of light and scent and sound. Aurelie's heart caught at the beauty the Fae trailed behind them like another floating drapery. In their presence it was impossible to think of war, of treachery or mistrust. It smacked of betrayal, setting aside the Heir's mantle like a heavy garment unsuited to the Fae world's warmth, but she told herself it was just for one last night. Loic didn't deserve to be abandoned a second time without explanation. It would only confirm his jaundiced view of mortals.

Coal-eyed Helis snatched the case from Aurelie's bedside table. "Bring your flute!"

"Come with us," Gaelle said. Her garment shimmered grass-green, her eyes gleamed, twin golden disks. Twiggy fingers smoothed Aurelie's hair, easing her headache. She followed the Fae through the opening in the floor and down the stairs into darkness. But the way to their realm was never hidden for long. At Helis's gesture, a wash of liquid light splashed ahead of them down a long staircase and against high walls. A tunnel of worked stone gave way to arches of folded rock, and then the grotto where her host waited. Piles of gold and silver coins and unset gemstones dotted the ground around him, like mulch heaps waiting to be spread over a garden. It was a sight to make a Skoeran trader weep.

As ever, the drac seemed indifferent to it, his compelling blue gaze fixed on Aurelie's face. The drac wore human shape, a suit of military cut, and boots polished to a high gloss. Seizing her hand, Loic drew her through another door and into the forest, where a crowd of Fae bowed with the whispering wind. She ran to keep up as her partner guided her in a complicated pattern between the other dancers. Collisions threatened at every turn, but the drac lifted them away, usually at the last possible moment. Loic's spirits were pitched fever-high and he capered like a lutin. Between his mischief and the wild dancing, it didn't seem the time for serious conversation.

Squealing and hiding her eyes from the tangle of dancers they left in their wake, Aurelie clutched Loic's shoulders. He held her closer still. Before she noticed her feet had left the ground, Aurelie was flying. Her slippers scuffed the treetops.

It was so wrong for Netta to miss this rapturous freedom! She belonged here in Loic's arms. Netta would be happy with the drac, while Aurelie's thoughts were fixed on another.

Under her feet, the stars flashed by, constellations turning as lazily as water lilies in a garden pond. Faster and faster they danced, traversing the night sky like a comet, until the heavens spun around them. When Loic guided her to the earth, his expression serious for a change, Aurelie opened her mouth. Before she could gather breath to speak, Helis darted forward.

With an imperious gesture, the foxy lutine handed Aurelie her flute. "Play, Princess!"

Aurelie sighed and curtsied her thanks to Loic. Her prepared speech must be delayed again, lest Helis stick her pointed nose in Aurelie's affairs. She tapped her foot twice on the moss and blew into the instrument. A sea chantey rollicked out of the flute. Fae folk gathered around her, swaying to the music.

Inevitably, the Skoeran tune reminded Aurelie of Garin. Where was he? Shivering in a hidey-hole someplace? Hungry? Alone? He couldn't be more frightened than she was on his behalf. As she couldn't in daytime, Aurelie let the dark emotion possess her. It rose from deep inside and flowed out of her flute into the night.

She played the fear of the rabbit, hiding from the owl. She played the fear of every hunted thing, chased from its home. She played the mortal fears of losing those most dear, of making the wrong choices, of failure and betrayal. Notes whispered and gibbered and moaned out of the flute. She played her fear like a half-mad horse she must ride, clinging to its back while it trampled the timid corners of her soul. With her last scrap of breath, Aurelie blew a long, quavering note and then collapsed, sobbing, into Loic's arms.

The other Fae clustered around her, honeybees to their queen. Layers of iridescent color brushed against Aurelie's arms, her back, her feet. Rich as incense, the perfume of their skin overwhelmed her. She couldn't read the message in their jeweled eyes. Her fingers trembled. The flute dropped to the ground.

Helis rubbed her face against Aurelie's wrist. The black eyes glittered. "Delicious."

"Manners, madame," Loic said sternly.

Whining like a scolded pup, the lutine cringed and backed away. The spell drawing the others to Aurelie dissolved. With soft murmurs of approval, they separated from her side.

Gaelle stretched like a cat and bent to retrieve the flute. "Fear," the Fée Verte said, as if she still tasted it in the air. "You haven't played that for us before."

Aurelie wiped her eyes with her sleeve. "It wasn't music."

"Don't apologize for your gift." Loic's arms tightened around her waist. The drac sounded too intent. What had he done while she was weeping? Stuck her feet together? Dropped crickets in her hair?

Planted a betrothal ring on her finger?

He wouldn't have! Alarmed, Aurelie shifted her weight, ran a hand through her hair, and inspected her fingers. All seemed in order. "You enjoyed it?" she said. "I didn't know it would please you."

"Oh, ho." Helis had crept back to them. "Hiding more, Princess?"

Aurelie smothered the prickle of guilt. She wasn't hiding Netta; Netta was hiding herself. "Not at all," she said, but the glib response sounded flat. Aurelie had made a mistake and needed to fix it. Fear was part of her resolve: the fear she might have driven Garin away. If she saw him again, she owed him the candor she herself wanted.

"Lies!" The lutine leaped at a tree, snapping at nothing. "Human lies and spies!"

"I'm not spying! Loic told me to wait here," a voice protested. Helis dragged a brown-haired, green-eyed man from behind the tree.

"You!" Aurelie slid from Loic's arms to confront Garin. She seized the shabby black robe, lest he disappear as mysteriously as he had arrived. Of the emotions warring within her, anger escaped first. "Beast! Sneak! Why didn't you come out before? We've been so worried about you!"

"Funny way of showing it," Garin said. "Dancing and carrying on."

"Weren't you listening?" Irritation roughened the drac's mellow voice. "Perhaps you require new ears. Owl, or lynx?"

Farfadets and lutins melted into the shadows. Helis retreated behind a tree. Gaelle alone lingered, holding Aurelie's flute across her palms like an offering.

"I heard you scare her half to death." With his thumb, Garin wiped the tear tracks from Aurelie's face. "Don't cry, Your Highness. You and Netta are worth ten of this overgrown lizard."

"Overgrown!" Loic huffed.

"I was frightened for *you*," Aurelie said. More tears welled up, as if she'd been storing them for this occasion. "How did you escape from Skoe?"

He stepped away from her. "After I set the fire that ruined my family and arranged for your men to be blamed for it, you mean?"

His flippant tone dried her tears. "I mean," she said, "that you have friends who believe you innocent, no matter what the Skoeran council ruled. Friends who would help, if you could shape that stubborn tongue into asking."

"Your pardon." He rubbed his face. "I've not slept much, lately."

"Well, we have that in common." Aurelie sat on the moss. "Tell us what you think happened, and we'll share what we know."

His legs folded under him. "The warehouse blaze was set ahead of time, with a fuse, to make it appear like a dud firework. I think Captain Inglis did it, first paying two of your sailors to walk by so she could stoke bad feelings against your party and lure you into a trap. When that failed, she bribed the council's investigator to say I had tried to destroy her share of the cargo. Supposedly, I miscalculated the amount, blew up the warehouse, and set fire to the ships. She lost the merchandise, but her partners—my parents—owed her for it, so she still came out well ahead of them."

"Devious," the drac said.

"Don't tell me you approve," Aurelie said.

"I said it was clever, not that I approved," Loic clarified.

Aurelie turned to Garin. "Why would she do such an evil thing?"

"My guess is that Captain Inglis wanted to put my parents in debt to her and weaken their influence on the council. They've always held out for peace. If she could discredit them, fewer would object to the war plans."

"But she was born here," Aurelie said. "A Dorisen seamstress told me. Her oldest son, too. What turned them against us?"

"That's another odd thing," Garin went on. "My parents said she and young Hui arrived in Dorisen with a purse full of gold and the clothes on their backs. Jacinthe invested in the riskiest ventures, but not one failed. The right cargo at the right time, on the right route, with the right wind, as if heaven itself smiled on her. Married an influential trader named Inglis, and now all of Skoe's in her pocket."

"A gold purse and a suit of clothes, eh?" Loic mused. "Clever, ruthless, and absurdly lucky. Named Jacinthe. What does she look like?"

"My height," Aurelie said. "Pale blond hair and the most unusual light eyes, almost colorless. Her son has them, too."

Loic coughed. "Sounds like my old nurse."

"Your nurse?" Garin and Aurelie stared at him in disbelief.

"Fair Jacinthe." The drac bared his teeth. "Hair white as ice and a disposition a thousand times colder. That woman deserved every trick I played on her, I assure you. She had a son, you say?"

"Hui," Aurelie replied, her voice faint. It made a twisted kind of sense. Loic's nurse had been snatched from her family and made to look after a drac child, not knowing what had happened to her own son. Such a woman might well reclaim her son and flee to Skoe, holding a grudge against the king and countrymen who had failed to protect her from the capricious Fae.

"Hui." Loic tasted the name. "He should thank me for sparing him seven years of his mother's ill humor."

"Most children prefer bad-tempered mothers to *no* mother," Aurelie said.

"Humans are irrational," Loic said. Before they could argue about it, Garin drew the next obvious conclusion.

"If she was your nurse, she can see your people? The Fae, I mean."

"Ointment in the left eye, same as you. Before, actually," the drac said. "She'd served a few years already when I met you three. Nurses are for very young dracs. But when she left us, I believe her purse contained several items that my father didn't mean to include with her wages. Perhaps I'll call on her myself, now that she's surfaced." Loic smiled at Aurelie and Garin like a kindly uncle. "Any other little mysteries I can solve for you, dear friends, before it's your turn to satisfy *my* curiosity?"

"Do you know a vouivre?" Garin said hastily.

"A what?" Aurelie asked.

"A vouivre!" Loic vanished from their sight and returned a moment later in his natural shape, upper part man and lower part lizard. His fists clenched. "Stay away from them. Spawn of a gargouille and a mortal, the most suspicious, combative females you can imagine. Great obvious jewel in their foreheads, convinced everyone they meet wants to steal it, even if he is merely admiring the facets. Try and rip your face off, simple misunderstanding."

"Well, someone succeeded with this one," Garin said. "Helm Burgida," he added for Aurelie's benefit, and pointed at his forehead. "There's supposed to be a jewel there, but she hasn't got it."

"Oh. In that case." The drac relaxed. "Harmless as a mortal. Without her Luck, a vouivre *is* a mortal, to all intents. Can't find her way back to our world, poor creature, and she'd be defenseless if she could."

As if distressed by the other Fae's loss, Gaelle joined the conversation. "Seven years, before the vouivre can claim it again," she added sadly. "If she can find it. They don't always, and then they age and die like mortals."

"Worse for the thief, though," Loic said. "If he doesn't surrender it on the prescribed day, the Luck turns sour."

"For another seven years?" Garin asked.

"For the rest of the unfortunate's life, however long it lasts," Gaelle answered.

Loic touched his forehead. "Quite a feat. I'd be tempted to shake the man's hand and say well done to whoever managed it."

Aurelie looked at Garin. "Jacinthe Inglis," she said, for both of them.

"Quite probably," Loic answered. "She would have had the nerve. And a well-planned escape route. That seems to have been the woman's specialty." The drac steepled his fingers. "Now, dear Aurelie, perhaps you could clarify one point for me."

"Yes?"

"It's about Netta," he said, his voice silky.

Garin raised his hands. "I didn't tell him."

The lizard tail swept across the moss. "Tell me what?"

Aurelie stiffened. She had meant to give him a hint, but not under interrogation. "What about her?"

"Is she well?" His politeness was exquisite.

"Yes," Aurelie said. As well as could be expected, for a person who cried for hours into her pillow, thinking no one would notice the dark circles under her eyes.

"But?" The drac's fin lashed his back; his claws extended.

An impressive sight, Aurelie conceded. "But what?"

"Don't be dense!" Loic snarled. "What's the matter with her?"

"She made me promise!" Aurelie told him, driven by a mix of pity and exasperation. Judging by the drac's agitation, he missed Netta as sorely as she pined for him. "If you want to know more, find her and ask her."

"That's what I said," Garin pointed out. "Didn't I, Loic?"

The drac roared so loudly even Aurelie stepped back. "Useless mortals," he hissed, sounding remarkably like Helis. Sparks crackled around him, and he disappeared.

"The revel's over," Gaelle said mournfully. She shook her leafy hair. "Come, I'll escort you to your room, Princess. Man."

"I can't go to the palace," Garin said.

"Oh, yes you can." Aurelie dragged Garin after the Fée Verte. She hoped Loic would find Netta soon; their reunion was long overdue. For her part, Aurelie had Garin back again. This time, war or no war, they'd get a few things straight before she let him go.

CHAPTER 20

Aurelie

But when Aurelie tapped on the sitting room door early the next morning, silence answered her.

Garin had left a folded blanket at the foot of the daybed and no other sign of his presence. He knew the palace as well as Netta and Aurelie; he could be anywhere.

She might have slept in, Aurelie thought, rather than troubling to get up and dressed before Elise had even come out of her room to build up the fires. As she refused to chase Garin through Lumielle, the princess marched around the Heir's Suite, thumping pillows to relieve her annoyance. She twitched open the heavy drapes and discovered a world transformed.

The snowstorm Netta predicted had turned the city into a confectioner's masterwork. White icing frosted the garden's hedge maze, fountains, and trees. The statues on Tower Bridge wore tall white caps like pastry chefs. Beyond, creamy drifts obscured the bags of earth piled against the city walls, the cannons and balls, and the rest of the ugly preparations for war. After dropping their cargo of snow, the clouds had sailed on. The sun rose in a clear sky to dazzle people emerging from their snowbound houses. As the bundled figures swept steps and paths clear, Aurelie marshaled her thoughts.

Jacinthe Inglis had been Loic's nurse. Aurelie was still grappling with the idea that the Skoeran captain had cared for the baby drac. Though, according to Loic, "cared for" wasn't the best description of her actions. But it did explain some things, like the way Hui had reacted to the mention of Cantrez. His memories of the place where his mother had been stolen couldn't be happy ones. Strange to think that Aurelie might have seen him playing with the other children at the Longest Day celebrations. The royal household had often celebrated the summer festivities in the town of Queen Basia's birth. It hurt to know that some who had shared her childhood home had turned so bitterly against Jocondagne.

The revelation also raised new concerns. If Captain Inglis could see the Fae, thanks to the drac's ointment, then she must know Burgida's identity. So why had the Skoeran hired her to helm *Gargouille*? If Inglis had stolen the vouivre's Luck, perhaps she knew about the time limit and meant to surrender it. Or was there another reason to keep the magic stone's true owner close? Did Burgida's involvement have any bearing on the war with Jocondagne, or was it strictly a personal matter between Inglis and the Fae?

Aurelie came no closer to resolving any of it. She leaned against the cold glass and stared into the garden. Like a length of Netta's lace, snow-covered branches intertwined in delicate patterns against the brightening sky. A black streak in the distance caught her eye. A big dog—no, two dogs—raced through the garden toward the palace. White plumes feathered out behind them as their tails brushed clumps of wet snow off the bushes. Their trail looked like a careless cook had swished her spoon through lumpy pudding.

The dogs disappeared behind the hedge maze and then returned to pass directly under Aurelie's window. The larger dog grinned at her over his shoulder. A rope of sausages dangled from his jaw. Aurelie laughed at his comical expression, then squinted.

Loic?

She leaned her elbows on the sill and craned her neck. Before the running dogs turned the corner of the building, Aurelie was convinced that the second dog was Loic, and the first, Netta. She thought she knew where they were headed, too: the gap between the kitchen garden wall and a row of evergreens. Netta, Aurelie, and Garin used to meet there to share treats smuggled from the kitchen.

Aurelie pulled on her boots and coat. The solicitous Barret wasn't on duty this early, but another sleepy-looking footman wished Aurelie good morning and opened the door. He didn't ask her any questions or offer to fetch her a cape. The cold air nipped at her face as she scuffed through the snow, following the track the dogs had made.

Sure enough, it led to the row of evergreens. Halfway along, Aurelie met Netta, in her own shape, sidling out from between two trees. Netta's expression was so radiant, the heat of it could have melted the snow clinging to her brown hair.

"Psst!" Aurelie said. "Over here."

If anyone deserved happiness, Netta did. So why did Aurelie's insides clench a little when she read the joy on Netta's face?

"Aurelie!" She hurried forward, her coat dusted with snow from the evergreen branches. When the blind girl would have continued past Aurelie, the princess reached out to stop her. Netta grabbed her by both hands and swung the two of them around until Aurelie was dizzy.

"Stop!" Aurelie said.

Netta let her go. Alone, she twirled down the path.

A load of snow slid off a tree and plopped at Aurelie's feet. Another soggy handful struck her back. "This way!" Aurelie said, chasing after her friend and steering Netta along the short path to the greenhouse.

Inside, they stood between shelves of plants too delicate to winter outside. The humid warmth melted the white flakes from their coats and caressed their cold faces. Surprisingly, the two girls had the place to themselves. Aurelie had expected to see people tending to the plants and feeding the wood stoves that heated the building. Either it was too early or the gardeners were all busy in the palace, hanging evergreen garlands to bring the scent of the forest indoors for the festival.

"Lovely." Netta turned in place, less giddily.

Aurelie breathed in the rich smells of earth and green things that defied the cold white world outside. Would Netta tell her what she'd been doing? Or were they still keeping secrets from each other? "You're up early," she said, leaving her friend to decide.

"He found me." Netta's voice was hushed with wonder.

"Loic?" Aurelie said.

Netta's seeking hand met a fern. She stroked the frond uncurling at its base. "Isn't it funny—I smelled him, in my room. Wet earth, like here, and river reeds and musk. I said his name, and he answered."

"And then," Aurelie prompted.

Netta blushed. "Well, it was awkward at first. I told him how sorry I was not to see him, and he said that dawn would come soon. And I had to explain, you know, what I meant. What his father had done. And how ashamed I'd been for acting so stupidly...."

"But he understood," Aurelie said, when Netta's voice trailed away.

"Yes. He forgave me for not telling him. And then I forgave him for kissing you, Aurelie." Netta screwed up her face in a determined expression. "That's to stop, Your Highness. Loic and I won't be parted again."

"Am I pardoned, too?" Aurelie asked.

Netta cocked her head, considering. Water dripped, loud in the silence. "Yes," she said, and her fierceness softened into a smile. "So all our forgiving took a while, and at the end of it, Loic said that although he couldn't reverse my blindness, he could transform me into other shapes with eyes that work. We were dogs this morning, just splendid! He's learned the most amazing magic, Aurelie. You never said."

"I don't think he told me the half of it."

"Mm." Netta smiled and walked among the shelves, identifying plants by touch and scent. Aurelie guided her away from the thorny rose bushes to the softer geraniums. The blind girl plucked a fuzzy leaf and crushed it between her fingers, releasing the scent of mint and chocolate. "I'm so glad Garin escaped from Skoe. But that dreadful Captain Inglis was Loic's nurse! She was paid handsomely for her trouble, wasn't she? I can't understand why she's bent on fighting us."

"Well—" Aurelie said, but Netta had marched into the next aisle and was sniffing a pot of faded narcissus.

"Loic says she's a cold, vengeful woman. He'll stand with us against her when the time comes." She whirled. "Can you imagine, a drac getting involved in a human quarrel?"

"For your sake?" Aurelie said dryly. "I have no trouble believing that of Loic."

Netta's cheeks turned pink. She ducked her head. "I missed him so much, Aurelie. It's my dearest dream come true, finding him again and feeling closer even than before."

"That's wonderful," Aurelie said wistfully.

"It's the same with you and Garin, isn't it?"

"Oh." Aurelie tried for a laugh, but it sounded defeated. "We're never in one place together long enough to decide."

"But Loic said he left Garin with you last night."

"Gone again this morning."

Netta tucked her hand in Aurelie's arm. "We'll find him at breakfast."

"I suppose so," Aurelie said.

"I know so," Netta retorted. "Eggs and sausage and toast and apple butter, after eating nothing but fish for months and months? He'll be there, don't worry."

CHAPTER 21

Aurelie

Aurelie shredded a butter pastry between her fingers as Garin worked his way through a third plateful. The Skoeran appeared capable of consuming every dish the cook cared to prepare. She was so delighted at his return that only her festival preparations kept the woman from running through her entire repertoire at his first meal.

Though less demonstrative, King Raimond also seemed gratified that Garin had sought refuge in Jocondagne. The two of them had arrived in the dining room together, after Aurelie had let several cups of tea go cold, waiting, and Netta had already excused herself.

"You're always welcome here, Deschutes," the king had said for the benefit of several courtiers casting dubious looks at Garin's wild hair and foreign clothing. "We'll sort out those ridiculous allegations with the rest of the Skoeran situation, won't we, Aurelie?"

"Yes, Papa."

Her father stopped by her chair and spoke softly. "Do get him some decent clothes, daughter. With invasion on the city's mind, folk will be suspicious of strangers. We wouldn't want any trouble because of our friend's Skoeran, er, fashions."

"No, Papa."

"Your festival dress is ready too, isn't it?"

"Yes, Papa."

"Good, good." The slate-blue eyes studied her. Aurelie stiffened in her chair, wondering what he and Garin might have discussed during their private interview. But the king changed the subject. "Master Austringer speaks highly of your work with the sea eagles. We're looking forward to the ceremony tomorrow, very much."

Aurelie relaxed. "For wild birds, he says, they've come along amazingly fast."

"Excellent." With an approving nod, the king took his seat, and the first adviser approached to confer with him. The servants might be occupied with preparing for tomorrow's festival, but at the king's table, war dominated the conversation. How many ships the Skoerans might launch, the troop strength each side could muster, whose plans the spring winds might favor. She'd heard the same questions debated every day for weeks, but not with Garin there. Aurelie squirmed in her chair. How must he feel?

Nothing showed in his face. Garin ate, hardly looking up from his plate. When the king finished, the room emptied quickly, leaving only Garin and Aurelie. He pushed his empty plate to one side and stretched. "Your mission is to civilize me, I hear? Redress the scurvy Skoeran?"

"Yes," she said. His flippant tone didn't fool her. He'd had a long journey, only to find himself among enemies. Not that Aurelie was one, but...Daylight illuminated lines in his face that she hadn't noticed the previous night. She wiped her buttery hands on her napkin, not sure how to act around him. Before she could decide, the door flew open and banged against the wall.

Aurelie jumped. Garin slid out of his chair so smoothly she almost missed the flash of steel. A knife slid out of his boot, then back when he recognized the plump woman rushing at him.

Netta's mother engulfed him in a warm embrace. "Garin! My dear boy, how tall you've grown!"

Her daughter stood in the doorway. "Mother insisted on coming down the instant she heard."

"You haven't changed a bit, madame," Garin said. "But your daughter's grown much prettier." He released the seamstress and bent over Netta's hand.

"Why, thank you, Monsieur Impertinence!" Netta reached up to tug his ear and her fingers brushed the elf-braids. "Traveling with lutins, Garin?"

"Hush, child!" Her mother glanced around the room.

Just when Aurelie was feeling left out of their teasing exchange, Garin dropped her a wink behind the older woman's back. "I've been keeping much more exalted company," he said.

Netta smirked. "Really?"

"Oh, aye."

Her mother examined him over her spectacles. "I don't know about foreign standards, but here in Lumielle, you'll wear better than that shabby excuse for a robe, so help me."

"You're very kind, madame," Garin said.

Aurelie was becoming quite desperate to get him out of the palace, away from all the old friends who might be lining up in the corridor to greet him. "How about skate blades?"

"What a good idea," Netta chimed in. "Don't you have one more session with Master Austringer? While you two are out there, you can test the course before the races tomorrow."

"A skating costume?" The older woman beamed at Garin. "It's no trouble to fit you, no trouble at all. Come with me. You can meet the princess at the stables within the hour. Will that suit, Your Highness?"

"Yes," Aurelie said. Returning to her room, she changed into a tunic and leggings, coat, hat, scarf, and gloves. She hurried, but Garin was ready before her, dressed in Jocondagnan blue and admiring the two bay mares and their string of silver bells.

The sleigh driver cracked the long whip over his head, and the mares trotted through the palace gates. Teams of supply sledges had already packed the snow; the sleigh moved easily through the crowded streets. In addition to the capital's usual activity, many people were returning from the countryside with armfuls of greenery. Children headed out of the city with their sleds and skate blades. At the southernmost King's Gate, Aurelie answered the guards' salutes with a wave, and they left the city walls behind.

Sunlight sparkled off the snow covering farmers' fields and grazing meadows alike. The frozen expanse of the river's main channel shone blue-white where the freshening wind had scoured snow from the ice. On the wide loop of the skating course, sheltered from the breeze by a ring of snow-encrusted pine, willow, and chestnut trees, sweepers moved in even ranks across the ice. Hammer blows echoed from the island inside the course.

The way to the festival grounds seemed even busier than Lumielle's streets. Sleighs and sledges carried construction materials, wood for the bonfires, and supplies for the cook tents. Then the sleigh stopped with a jolt, throwing Aurelie and Garin against the seat back.

"Your pardon, Highness." The driver pointed with his whip. "Carter's spilled a load of firewood across the track. That'll take a while to clear."

Aurelie was in no mood to sit still. "Let's walk," she said. The two of them left the sleigh and pushed through the snow to cross the frozen River Sicaun where the ferry docks would be in summertime. In warmer weather, this island was a pretty picnic spot shaded by the ring of trees. Now a temporary city was rising like a stage set from the snow. Tents displayed a variety of craft guilds' wares. Teams of workers assembled tables and benches, and a long line of metal spits stood waiting to roast meat for the feast.

Aurelie led them to the red-draped reviewing stand. Her father and Master Austringer would stand here for the king's part of the sea eagle ceremony while she and Dalfi, the assistant falcon keeper, waited on Tower Bridge. She looked around. "I don't see Master Austringer yet. He brings the fish for our practice."

"Shall we skate, then?" Garin said, and Aurelie nodded.

Down the hill from the reviewing stand, wooden benches had been placed along the riverbank. Aurelie and Garin sat and threaded leather straps through the metal plates and buckles, then attached the blades to their boots. As Aurelie stood up, one fashionably dressed young woman stumbled. Squealing, she slid into another girl and knocked them both into a heap. Aurelie was thankful not to be wearing layers of frothy skirts. If she fell, she wouldn't look quite so much like an overturned feather-duster.

"Ready?" Garin said.

"Yes." Aurelie pushed off with one blade. She wobbled, threw her arms out for balance, then straightened.

Push, glide. Push, glide.

The sweepers had started in the middle of the Sicaun and were working outward toward the edges, leaving a long, clear track down the course. As her confidence mounted, Aurelie's strokes picked up speed. Soon she was flying over the ice, Garin a silent shadow at her elbow. Skating, they didn't need to speak, to apologize, to explain. They moved side by side in perfect accord.

Garin's blades rasped against the ice. He shot forward, a challenge. Aurelie coasted in his draft. She wasn't worried about losing. She'd spent day after day working with the sea eagles, night after night dancing with Loic. Her legs were strong, her muscles warming up, loose and ready. The important thing was to find a steady rhythm. When the Skoeran tired of setting the pace, she'd pass him.

Her world condensed to the view of Garin's blue coat in front of her, the scrape-scrape of metal blades against the ice, the drafts of cold air sucked down her throat and expelled in clouds of vapor. This silent communion was just what she'd needed. They belonged together, whether he knew it or not.

When his breath sounded harsher and more ragged, Aurelie acted. Swift as a swallow, she darted to one side. Wind shoved at her chest, but rather than stand up to it, Aurelie bent her body forward, clasped her hands behind her back, and let her legs do their work. Stride for stride, Aurelie matched Garin. Imperceptibly, she gained ground. He skated harder. Aurelie could sense that he was close enough to lock elbows, but she kept her eyes forward, on the red-draped reviewing stand. They'd almost completed the loop around the island; the striped finish wands awaited.

Slower skaters had moved out of their way. Aurelie quickened her pace again, enjoying the sound of Garin puffing behind her. She could skate with him all day, she thought, and never need to speak.

And then her right skate blade caught on a twig frozen into the ice. She tripped, lost her balance, and fell, sliding across the ice like a wind-driven leaf. By accident, one leg knocked Garin's skates out from under him. He landed on his back and followed her into the snowbank. At the double impact, the willow tree above them dropped its heavy, wet burden on their heads.

Coughing and spluttering snow, Aurelie pushed herself upright. "Tie!" she declared.

"What?"

At Garin's outraged expression, she doubled over with laughter. His hat had come off. Snow crusted his braids, and he was scooping more of the white stuff out of his collar. "Best of three," he said.

"No, that's enough skating, thank you."

"You want to talk, I suppose? Girls always do."

Her temper fired. "In Dorisen, you wouldn't tell me anything! Why you were disguised, the business with Captain Inglis... I could have helped! I wanted to!"

Garin retrieved his hat and shook it, hard. "While you cozied up to Hui Inglis?"

"That was diplomacy." Aurelie waved away his objection. "It didn't mean anything."

"Would you have taken that chance?"

"Yes," she said, instantly. "I would have trusted you. I did trust you, remember?" She slapped her gloves together. "Didn't admit I knew you. Didn't blab your name to anyone. Chose your box-chair, not one of Inglis's, when the mob was coming. Tell me the real reason you kept pushing me away."

Garin jammed his hat on his head. "Because I was afraid," he said bluntly. "You're a princess, and I'm a merchant's son. Now a sail mender and plank caulker's son. We hadn't spoken in over two years; our countries were at war. What if you believed the Inglises over me?"

"Are you joking? Not believe you? You're my oldest friend, with Netta and Loic!"

"Loic." His face went wooden. "So you're going to marry him?"

"That's not what I said!" Tears of frustration burned her eyes. "Forget it. Let's talk about something else."

"No." Garin's glove touched her sleeve, then dropped to his side. "I have to know. Do you love him?"

"Who, *Loic*?"

"I wouldn't stand between you," he said in a low voice. "An accused criminal can't offer much, not like a drac, with his magic and all. I saw you dancing together last night. And, um," he finished like an unwound clock.

Aurelie glared at him while her ears caught up with her brain. She'd watched Netta listening, comparing what people said with how they said it. Her blind friend didn't read minds, as Aurelie had once imagined. She listened.

Garin's words told her "go ahead and marry someone else," but his voice implied the opposite.

"I do enjoy dancing with Loic," Aurelie enunciated. "He's an old friend, as I said, and crazy about Netta, which you also might remember. I happen to *love*, love, a blockheaded person who still hasn't trusted me with the complete truth."

"What?"

Aurelie folded her arms into wings, and flapped them up and down. "Bawk, bawk," she said, as rudely as she could. She wanted to provoke him; this self-effacing meekness didn't suit Garin at all.

"You love *me*?"

"For a clever Skoeran, you can be very stupid."

The gray-green eyes narrowed. "Who's so brave, slinging insults instead of saying what she means?"

"Fine." Aurelie leaned forward and tapped his chin with her glove. "I"—*tap*—"love"—*tap*—"you." *Tap*. "Is that clear?"

"*Love*, love, or..."

When Aurelie pulled her own hair in frustration, he wrapped his arms around her. "Sorry. I couldn't resist."

"Garin?" Aurelie licked her cold lips. "I want to hear it."

"I." He kissed her left eyebrow. "Love." He kissed her right eyebrow. "Princess." He kissed her nose.

"Me," she said, and claimed his lips. Eventually, she remembered they were sitting in a pile of snow next to a busy skating course. "What are we going to do?"

"You have a nice long name, including the honorifics," he said. "House Pygargue, Heir to the Throne, Friend of Dracs, Confronter of Cowards....I figured I'd work my way through the list."

"Plenty of time for that, monsieur," she said primly, then giggled at his expression. "I mean," she repeated, some time later, "what are we going to do about Captain Inglis?"

"Nothing, at the moment." He kissed her nose. "Festival's tomorrow, spring still weeks away. We'll worry about Inglis later."

CHAPTER 22

Aurelie

The festival gown glittered like a column of ice. Aurelie stood at the top of Tower Bridge's central tower and swished her heavy skirts from side to side, enjoying the effect. The gold rays of the setting sun flickered from a hundred tiny mirrors sewn to the white satin overdress. As she moved, sparks of light danced across Lumielle's rooftops.

Garin was stamping down snow. After the storm, guards had swept a path just inside the tower's parapet so watchers could patrol the wall. The snow in the center of the roof had formed a thin crust over icy granules, making it a chore to walk through.

"Ack," Garin said, as bright spots flashed over his face. "You're blinding me!"

"Close your eyes," Aurelie retorted.

"As you command, Highness." Garin turned his face expectantly toward her.

Aurelie laughed. Her back to the distant festival grounds, she crossed the tower roof and dropped a kiss on his waiting lips. When he would have stolen another, she flitted out of reach. "Dalfi's coming with more fish buckets."

"But it's the first time we've been alone in hours," Garin said.

"Alone?" Aurelie laughed again. "There's a company of soldiers on the bridge below us, and way up here we're visible from all over the city. More soldiers at the gates and on the walls—they're all watching, aren't they? Not to mention Loic and Netta, wherever they are."

"Dogs, or crows, or what?"

Aurelie searched the sky. "I don't see them."

"Wish Loic would give us a turn," Garin grumbled.

"I think we're a little too visible today. We'd be missed."

"Tomorrow, then," Garin said. "Or the next day. I'd like to be a dog for an afternoon."

"Me, too." Aurelie hugged her elbows, as if the happiness welling inside her might spill out. Tomorrow or the next day. Such delicious words!

She did a little jig, to watch the reflections play over the snow. With Garin beside her, the shortest day of the year had flown by. Next came the event she had worked toward for weeks. Before the sun touched the horizon and the feast began, Master Austringer would call the sea eagles to the reviewing stand on the island, and then Aurelie would whistle them to her. She couldn't wait to see the spectacle from on high, the birds circling between island and city, king and Heir, their white wings catching the sun like pieces of her mirrored dress.

The assistant falcon keeper clumped up the tower stairs and set two pails of fish next to the others. "Princess Aurelie, you look beautiful."

"Thank you, Dalfi." Aurelie curtsied. "You're very fine yourself."

"New coat." He grinned at Garin and ducked down the stairs again, returning with more buckets and two large leather gauntlets. "Here, Your Highness."

Aurelie held out her sparkling arms and Dalfi strapped the gauntlets over the mirror-encrusted sleeves. "One more thing." He ran down the stairs again for a wooden stool. "If you get tired of standing."

"So, Dalfi." Garin had started in the center and was stomping in a spiral pattern, Aurelie noticed, around and around like a seashell. "Did you bring any snacks? To keep our strength up."

"Fresh whitefish?" The falcon keeper pulled a hatchet out of his belt. "I can chop it finer."

"Nah, I like mine cooked," Garin said.

Aurelie paced to the southeastern side of the tower and stared in the direction of the festival grounds. "Too bad the trees block our view of the finish line. We'll miss the final races."

"We can hear 'em, though," Dalfi said. "Horns signal the last lap. Then the king awards the winners and they'll call the eagles down. We're ready in good time. The birds, too, lookit." He pointed with his hatchet. "There's Paumera and Montbrai, Carbonnel and Orbec."

Aurelie watched the war birds soar past. "They know they're first, don't they?"

"Free supper, you can count on Montbrai at the head of the line."

"I know some people like that," Aurelie said.

"Hey," Garin protested. Dalfi chuckled.

Aurelie perched on the stool and whistled under her breath, running through the commands. *Monter, plonger, au tour.* Garin prowled around the tower wall. He'd been up since early morning, helping Aurelie through the day's pageantry in a hundred unobtrusive ways. She knew his presence was what had really made the day special. No receiving line seemed too endless, no task too daunting with Garin beside her and Netta and Loic nearby. Whatever shape they wore.

In the past few hours, the fear Aurelie had carried since the failed negotiations in the fall had dropped from her heart, a burden she no longer needed to carry alone. With companions like hers, who needed to steal a magic jewel? The four of them would make their own luck.

Perhaps, Aurelie thought, the turning season had something to do with her newfound hope. The Longest Night was one of the two hinges of the year. As it closed, Aurelie fancied she could taste her fortune changing, like the tang of salt that laced the chill breeze.

She snuggled her chin deeper into her collar and joined Garin at the shoulder-high wall facing the sea end of the frozen River Sicaun. He sniffed the air. She wondered what it smelled like to him. Ocean? Whitefish? Home?

"A lot of tall masts out by the breakwater," he said.

Aurelie shaded her eyes against the glare. "Twenty or thirty, at least."

"There were only three or four oceangoing ships when I came in. Did your father expect more Jocondagnan vessels for the festival?"

"I don't know." Aurelie gulped air, and the salt taste flooded her mouth with bitterness. That quickly, the fear returned. Her wool underdress, leggings, and boots might as well have been made from the same thin stuff as her mirrored gown, so little did they protect her from the chill.

Too many ships. Someone at the palace would have mentioned their arrival, if only to work out the order in which the captains should be seated at table. A terrible certainty took shape within her. "You think they're Skoeran?" she said softly.

Garin pounded his fist against the wall. "Who'd start a siege in this weather?"

"Cold living, in tents," Aurelie agreed. "And they couldn't bring supplies, arms, explosives, and rams up the river like usual, because it's frozen."

"Unless..." Garin leaned forward and gripped the edge of the parapet, as if he were going to be sick over the side.

"Garin?" The expression in the gray-green eyes frightened her. "Unless what?"

"Unless they brought iceboats," he said.

"But the River Sicaun never freezes this early," Aurelie said. "Maybe once in a hundred years. They couldn't have counted on it."

"No?"

They stood so close together that she felt Garin's shudder along her body as the first sail bloomed in the distance. Like an out of season lily, white canvas petals unfurled. Then another popped open, and another. They looked so graceful, nodding silhouettes against the sun, but Aurelie knew the iceboats were poison flowers. Those steel runners would cut right through defenses mounted against a different kind of attack, and their untimely arrival signified death, not spring.

It didn't seem possible that this lovely day could end so abruptly in destruction. Was that the change she had smelled?

Now Aurelie was certain that Inglis had stolen Burgida's Luck. The Skoeran's timing was too perfect, catching the bulk of the king's forces at the festival grounds, the rest unprepared for armed ships on skates. Aurelie could hardly comprehend what must follow.

"Curse her," Garin said hoarsely. "I should have guessed she'd try this. I'm an idiot. Planking's too good for me. You should—"

"Stop it." Aurelie's fists curled inside the heavy gauntlets. "I saw iceboats in Dorisen, too, and didn't realize the threat. We have to warn my father. Tell the soldiers below to send a skater south to the festival grounds, and another upriver, where the boats will hit first. There are cannons mounted at Sea Gate; it's the first place Papa had reinforced. Maybe our side can hold long enough for people to get away from the island."

"Aye." Garin ran for the stairs.

Aurelie knew there wasn't much chance the message would arrive in time. A man's blades couldn't travel nearly as fast as an iceboat's. Long before they could hope for reinforcements, the Jocondagnans at Sea Gate would face the enemy.

"What's the matter with him?" Dalfi asked.

"Iceboats." Aurelie's lips didn't want to shape the word, but Dalfi needed to know. The three of them were trapped here, with one company of soldiers and no relief in sight. "Skoeran vessels."

The falcon keeper's face turned fish-belly white. "The invasion?"

"Yes," Aurelie answered.

Garin ran back up the stairs, his expression grim. "The guard captain understands." He joined Aurelie at the parapet. "White sails with a green stripe, that's *Rayonne.*" He shook his head as if he had trouble believing what he was seeing. "*Iceflash, Sea Wolf.* I don't recognize most of the others. Inglis must have had crews building frames around the clock."

Aurelie saw red sails. "Garin. It's not...not *that* boat?"

They stared at each other in mutual horror. If the dragon answered to her name, she could destroy the city!

"Inglis wants someone else to do her work for her?" Garin guessed.

"Loic won't like that. Netta said he'd stand with us."

"But he's no match for the other one." Neither Garin nor Aurelie would say the gargouille's name aloud.

The first iceboat glided down the frozen river to the northernmost Sea Gate. Cannons coughed from the city walls, the smoke visible before the noise traveled across the quiet city. "It's started," Aurelie whispered. "Look, there are soldiers at the gate."

"Too many of 'em, though," Dalfi groaned.

Skoerans, he meant. Men swarmed off the iceboat and engaged with the gate guard. Smaller guns fired, sharp pops at this distance. Aurelie felt each one in the pit of her stomach. From their vantage point at the top of the tower, it was like watching a play, except that at the end, the actors wouldn't be rising to take their bows. This was real.

Though outnumbered, the Jocondagnans fought bravely. They stopped the first crew and the next, but the third iceboat broke through, whipping south.

"Hey!" Garin leaned over the wall and shouted. "We need more men up here. That boat's got grappling hooks."

"Why?" Dalfi asked, as boots pounded up the stairs.

"So they don't need to control the door," Garin explained. "They'll climb straight up the tower walls to get to the princess."

Closer, now, the steel runners scraped the ice. Like skate blades, but louder. Garin wrapped his arms around Aurelie and kissed her. "For luck," he said.

She couldn't answer; her throat felt tight.

The iceboat approached the bridge. They were here. Time slowed for Aurelie, giving her a last golden moment to see the love and despair swimming in Garin's gray-green eyes. She touched a finger to his lips, the leather gauntlet heavy on her arm. Garin pulled the knife from his boot.

"I'll protect you too, Highness." Fear pinched Dalfi's face, but he hoisted a bucket and shook it. "They come over that wall, I'll knock 'em down!"

Aurelie found her voice. "Felled by fish, how appropriate."

The iceboat glided to a stop. Howling as they came, riggers swarmed up the bridge supports.

"Fish..." Aurelie looked up and saw that two eagles had joined the others. Netta and Loic. She waved at them. Together again, all four. For the last time, most likely. Tears threatened, and Aurelie squeezed them back, staring hard at the pale shapes drifting in the sky, like snow. "The war birds," she whispered. Pursing her lips, she whistled Paumera's call. One white eagle separated from the rest.

The first of the iron hooks clanged over the parapet. It bit against the stone coping, and held. Line hissed through the ring at the end, chain jangling after. A soldier tried to dislodge it, but the opposing crewman's weight kept the chain taut. Another soldier leaned over the wall and fired.

"Don't throw your bucket, Dalfi. We'll need the fish." Aurelie reached into the pail, held up her arms and whistled again. *Plonger.* Paumera dropped out of the sky.

Another grappling hook pitched over the edge of the parapet, but its edge failed to catch. As it rasped along the tower roof, Dalfi hooked it with his hatchet and heaved it back over the wall. Aurelie braced herself. The eagle landed with a body-shaking thump on her right fist and took the offered tidbit in one swallow. Then, as if the great raptor knew the time had come to put her training to use, she lifted just far enough off the leather gauntlet to dive over the side of the tower, talons extended. In the next breath, Aurelie whistled for Montbrai. "Fish!" she said. Dalfi slapped another into Aurelie's left glove.

Paumera screamed. A man's shout ended in a horrible gurgle, followed by a muffled smack. Like a body hitting the ice under the bridge. Aurelie couldn't dwell on it. More Skoerans were coming. Jocondagnan soldiers dashed along the parapet, shooting at the climbing riggers. Hooks clanged, chain rattled, guns fired. Acrid smoke hung in the air.

For once, Montbrai didn't loll on Aurelie's glove, hinting for another reward. Instead, the great wings kept beating as the bird gulped the fish and flew to attack the enemies. Eagle Netta and eagle Loic hadn't waited to be summoned. They made an army of two, their talons slashing at the Skoeran riggers.

For Aurelie, the next little while was a blur of buffeting wings and slick whitefish, and whistling, and gunshots, and the screaming of eagles and men. Her job was to remember the notes that summoned each of the war birds. She was aware of Garin, never far from her side, of Dalfi, knocking chains away with his hatchet, then packing empty buckets with snow and hurling them onto the climbing men.

The invaders had the inexorable power of numbers. As more and more iceboats arrived, Aurelie's small force gave way, step by hard-fought step, until the Jocondagnan soldiers below the tower roof had been captured, wounded, or killed. Those fighting with her ran out of ammunition and were shoved downstairs to join their fellow prisoners.

Aurelie, Garin, and Dalfi found themselves back to back in a tight circle in the center of the roof. To scatter her aerial defenders, Aurelie had whistled a last *monter*. She didn't want the eagles to come within gun range. The Skoerans shot at the birds but were evidently under orders not to kill her. Royal hostages must be more valuable alive than dead.

Eagle Loic, however, had a fine sense of the weapons' capabilities against his own speed and power. The first few men who had tried disarming Garin or reaching for the princess had staggered away, deep furrows bleeding from the back of their heads. The rest kept their distance, content to wait for their commander's instructions.

Aurelie took a deep breath. Sweat cooled on her neck and back. Her arms ached from the weight of the gauntlets. Dalfi, trembling behind her, seemed safe but Garin's jacket sleeves were slashed. He tied a torn-off strip above his left elbow, pulling it tight with his teeth.

"Can I help?" she asked.

"This'll do," Garin said. "You're not harmed?"

"No." Aurelie rubbed her cold face before realizing that fish scales covered the glove. She thought briefly that Helis would enjoy the joke. Princess Fishface. But still, a princess, and Jocondagne's Heir. The thought straightened her back and lifted her chin. She had to secure Garin's safety, and Dalfi's. "What are your terms?" she asked the closest Skoeran. "I will require safe conduct for my men."

A stir by the stairs, and Captain Inglis strode onto the roof, immaculate in a gold jacket and crimson skirts. "You *require*?" she said, light eyes bright with victory. "Climbing a slippery rope, aren't you, little missy? And here's our lost Woolie, Helm," she called over her shoulder. "No use hiding behind a Jok's glass skirts, Deschutes."

Garin didn't respond to the taunt.

Burgida followed a silent Hui Inglis up the stairs and into their midst. As usual, the Fae's expression was solemn under her crown of red hair. An unhealthy green tinge colored the First's skin. His hand twitched, and his knife gleamed.

Aurelie refrained from suggesting he put the thing away before he cut himself. "We're all assembled," she said instead, ignoring the weakness in her legs. The stool was next to her, but she wouldn't sit while her enemy stood. "Suppose you tell us what you want, Jacinthe Inglis."

The mocking eyes surveyed the state of the princess's gown. Fish guts slimed the mirrors and the white fabric was creased and spotted, but Aurelie wouldn't have traded it for Inglis's red and gold.

"Aurelie, dearest," the captain said, her fawning tone more insulting than a slap. "A little courtesy, please, to your future mother."

Garin swore viciously under his breath. It shouldn't have been a surprise, but Aurelie felt the color drain from her face. She'd probably turned the same color as Hui. If they married, the Skoerans would claim Jocondagne's throne. So the raiders had planned only to kidnap Aurelie. Capturing the city was simply an unexpected bonus.

"No fool Jok's more predictable than a royal one," Captain Inglis sneered. "With your precious traditions, your white eagles, your other pretty monstrosities." She sent a venomous look skyward, where Netta and Loic circled out of reach. "Never trust them. Seven years of my life, lost to that horror."

Aurelie hated to let this woman see how frightened she was. She spoke as coolly as she could. "And the next seven? You don't seem to have done so badly for yourself."

"Clever girl." She simpered in a parody of admiration before her face closed. "You remember what we discussed, son?"

"Yes, Ma." Hui Inglis was sweating. He took a step away from his mother, closer to Helm Burgida. Aurelie didn't blame him. She didn't like the sudden hard set of the captain's features, as if now was the moment on which all else depended.

From under the gold jacket, the Skoeran woman tugged a fist-sized bag on a leather cord. The faceted jewel she withdrew from the bag gathered in the last remaining sunlight and shone like a small star.

"My Luck!" Burgida started forward, then stopped, crying out in pain.

"*My* Luck at present," Captain Inglis said.

At first, Aurelie didn't understand what had happened. Blinking away the jewel's dazzling afterimage, she saw Hui's hand twisting Burgida's arm behind her back. His knife rested across her throat.

"Don't move," he said hoarsely.

"Not as calm as he pretends," Garin murmured in Aurelie's ear. "His hand's shaking."

She nodded, watching the Fae. Without her Luck, a vouivre was supposed to be as fragile as any human woman. But Burgida's voice sounded disdainful when she spoke. "Are all mortals' promises so false? You accepted my service in exchange for my Luck's return on Longest Day."

"You'll have it," the captain assured her. "But before it's worthless to me, there's one more transaction I'd like to complete."

"What's that?" Aurelie asked, when it became clear the vouivre wouldn't.

"Why, we'll trade the creature herself." The shining jewel lit the captain's cold smile. "I believe Burgida's mother will pay handsomely for her return in one piece, rather than several. Yes, this is turning into quite the profitable venture, although the details were somewhat complex to arrange. Do hold still, Helm. Hui's knife is sharp enough to cut mortal skin."

"Her *mother*?" Garin said. "No, don't, she's a—"

"Gargouille!" Jacinthe Inglis shouted.

CHAPTER 23

Aurelie

CRACK!

The ice beneath the bridge splintered, shaking the tower and spilling iceboats and crew into the frigid water. Men screamed and struggled to reach the banks. Along its length, the River Sicaun shrugged, a giant snake shedding its icy skin. From the dark water, a streak of orange fire ascended, trailing clouds of steam.

Fireworks, was Aurelie's first incoherent thought. Would the rocket explode over their heads or *on* them? Then she saw two great metallic wings unfold and smelled the sandalwood and spice wind of the Fae world. Worse than fireworks, far worse. As she feared, the namesake iceboat had attracted the gargouille to the mortal world, close enough to answer Inglis's call.

"What? What is that?" Hui gasped. The others couldn't see the dragon, Aurelie realized. They could hear it and smell it, but the gargouille's fearsome beauty was invisible to them.

Too bad. If Hui knew what his mother had summoned, he might have dropped the knife. Instead he held it closer to Burgida's throat, as likely to cut her by accident as intent. Aurelie's neck tingled in sympathy, which gave her the idea. Why not try a diversion?

Without time to explain, Aurelie found Garin's hand and squeezed. He squeezed back and let go. She could feel him shifting his weight, ready for whatever move she made.

"Excuse me, First Inglis." She pitched her voice purposely low, to draw his attention from the furious clamor in the sky.

"What?" He swiveled toward her. Burgida made a distressed sound, but Aurelie focused on catching and holding the First's gaze.

"You know they *spread disease*," she said, meaningfully, as if it was a code the two of them shared. Then she glanced down at her collar and brushed at it the way Elise had in Dorisen, to tell him about the spider.

He recognized the words or the gesture. Reflexively, his knife hand flew up, almost slicing his ear. The other hand let go of his hostage to slap at his coat. In the instant before the First realized he'd been tricked, Garin dove for Burgida's legs. The vouivre went limp, and the two of them rolled away from Hui Inglis and through the snow to end up against the parapet.

Aurelie dragged Dalfi after them. Captain Inglis screamed abuse at her son, but by the time Hui recovered his balance, the princess and Garin shielded the Fae and the falcon keeper with their own bodies.

The other Skoerans had backed away from the walls, staring in fear at the snow, which swirled upward in the drafts from the dragon's wing beats. The giant creature swooped and hovered, so close to the tower that her hot breath lit the torches in their wall brackets. "Who summons Gargouille?"

Whether from terror at the ring of torches flaring simultaneously or the sonorous, disembodied voice, two of the Skoeran riggers broke. "She did," they shouted. Pointing at their leader, they fell face-first into the snow.

At the same moment, an eagle screamed in challenge. A white streak cut across the smoking torches. Aurelie recognized Loic, flying straight at Captain Inglis with his talons open. Like her son, the woman couldn't help her first reaction. Both hands went up to protect her face from the immediate threat.

Screaming at full voice, Loic passed her with a wingspan to spare. In a tricky bit of flying, eagle Netta plummeted at the same instant and plucked the Luck from Inglis's fingers. Aurelie held her breath, fearing that the speed of her friend's descent might slam her into the roof. A mighty flapping, followed by a couple of hops, enabled Netta to drop the jewel in Aurelie's outstretched palm. She closed her gloved fingers around the Luck.

The white feathers blurred, and Netta tumbled out of eagle shape to land next to Dalfi. "Mademoiselle Netta," he said, and fainted.

Without a word, Captain Inglis bolted down the stairs, abandoning her son, her men, and the grand scheme that had unraveled when her Luck finally went sour.

Dragon sight, however, was even sharper than an eagle's. With a thundering, brassy bugle, like a drum and horn combined, the gargouille stretched her serpentlike neck and belched flame at the base of the tower.

"Ma!" Hui screamed. "No, Ma!"

One of the riggers pulled the distraught First away from the parapet. Aurelie turned her face into Garin's coat, shuddering. He held her tightly.

"Shall I roast these others, too, daughter?" the gargouille's inhuman voice purred with predatory satisfaction. It was softer than before but still loud enough to hurt Aurelie's ears.

"No, Mother. I'd rather you didn't," Burgida called. Blood trickled in a dark line down her neck and over her red jersey as she left the shelter of the wall. "May I please have my Luck back, Your Highness?"

Aurelie could feel the warmth of the jewel through the leather gauntlet. She faced the Fae. "I remember I owe you a favor," she said slowly. "But Netta recovered it. She should have a say."

"You dare, mortal?" The gargouille's roar singed the hem of Aurelie's festival gown.

The remaining Skoerans scrabbled away from the fire and fled down the stairs, leaving the dazed Hui behind. Garin relieved him of his knife.

Netta shook her head. "Burgida helped you and Garin escape from Skoe," she said, her voice husky. "I owe her, too, for your safe return. If she's blind to her true home without her Luck—well, I know what that's like. She should have it."

Aurelie looked at Garin, who nodded, unsmiling. "We don't need it."

Aurelie agreed. But a princess thought first of her people, and the Luck was a powerful bargaining chip. "Helm Burgida, would your mother mind very much retiring again from Jocondagne?"

"For another hundred years, perhaps?" the vouivre said dryly.

"I've killed your enemy, eh, so I can shove off? Leave my cave and treasure for that upstart drac?" The gargouille's voice blared annoyance. "Careful, girl."

Aurelie's cold toes curled in her boots. Who was she to negotiate with a dragon on behalf of her country? Puny against the immortal's power, splattered with fish guts, and wet from melting snow, she didn't cut an impressive figure. But who else could do it? Not her father, not Count Sicard. Garin and Netta had already said what they thought. The choice rested with her.

Aurelie realized that, thanks to her friendship with Loic, she did know a few things about the Fae. They respected courtesy more than a show of force, for one thing. It was worth the risk, if it succeeded. And really, did she want to follow Inglis's example?

"Not at all, madame," Aurelie said. She made herself hand the Luck to Burgida without any conditions attached. "Your presence does us too much honor."

"Hah!" The dragon's laugh clanged, a bronze bell. Fire licked the night sky. "Suck-breath."

"Don't be difficult, Mother. Let's leave them in peace." Burgida kissed the jewel and put it to her forehead, where it blazed, then dimmed. Like a fruit rind splitting, the human form peeled away from the vouivre's true shape. Bat wings unfurled from a long, sinuous body. The jewel flashed between two dark eyes, sad no longer. "Thank you, Princess. Good-bye, friends." The smaller dragon leaped into the air, her voice ringing with joy. It had the same metallic echo as the gargouille's. "Fare you well."

"Good-bye." Three voices answered her.

No, four, Aurelie realized. Loic stood next to Netta, tall and proud in his drac shape. The fin on his back glimmered in the torchlight.

With another blast of spice and fruit and sulfur, the Fae vanished. Aurelie swayed in exhausted relief, and Garin wrapped his arms around her waist.

"Well flown, my heart," Loic complimented Netta. The drac directed his violet gaze at Garin. "I didn't happen to notice *your* contribution to the evening's success, friend, but I'm sure it was equally valuable."

Garin snorted. "Now who's a suck-breath?"

Netta giggled. Loic turned to Aurelie. "Most delicately handled, Princess. I couldn't have charmed old bronze-face better myself."

"We were lucky," Aurelie said, and leaned into Garin's embrace.

CHAPTER 24

Aurelie

In the park behind the cathedral, snowflakes sifted through the chestnut tree's bare branches and powdered an evergreen's skirts. Sitting with her back to an old oak, Jocondagne's Heir lifted her flute to her lips. A mountain round whistled out in lively counterpoint to the gray afternoon. Drawn by the music, lutins and farfadets stole closer. And not only Fae folk. Children gathered as well. Two boys and a girl, Aurelie thought, from the hissing whispers behind her. She'd glimpsed the school satchels dangling from mittened hands as the three of them dashed from tree to tree.

The snow thickened. It muffled all sound but Aurelie's music, until the icy flakes collecting on the flute convinced her to finish with a Skoeran song Garin had taught her, about sailing the sweet salt sea.

As he'd done, so recently, and would again in a month or two, if all went well. She knew from the letter he'd sent. The first Skoeran trader in two years had brought his letter to Lumielle, along with a welcome cargo of cocoa, cloth, and spices.

Aurelie had unfolded and refolded the letter so many times that the paper was soft, the inked line of kiss marks smudged into a long embrace. Garin missed her, he wrote. He'd thought of her every night aboard the flagship escorting the remains of the Skoeran fleet back to Dorisen. With Captain Inglis dead, Hui disgraced, and his family owing reparations, King Raimond had appointed Garin to explain to the council in Dorisen why the invasion had failed. He'd return to Lumielle soon, Garin promised, with a new delegation, to work out the peace. Until then, he hoped she'd remember him, *over the sweet salt sea.*

The last notes hung in the air as Aurelie wiped her flute dry with a cloth and returned it to the case. She knelt by the granite marker to pat the eagle and goat. "Until soon, Mama," she said. Jumping to her feet, she winked at a nearby lutine. The Fae peered through her braids, alarmed at first by the acknowledgment. Then, shyly, she grinned back.

Aurelie put on her gloves and brushed the snow from her coat. Walking briskly, she set off for the cathedral where Elise was waiting. Another banquet to attend tonight, this one in honor of the surviving Jocondagnan defenders, but first Aurelie had decided to steal a few moments for herself.

A snowball lofted past her and splattered against a chestnut tree. Aurelie reacted, sidestepping a bush and dropping to her knees behind a pine tree. She scooped loose snow into her glove, waited until she heard giggling, then let fly.

"Hit! He's hit!" a shrill voice cried. "That's one for the girls!"

Snow exploded, cold and wet, against Aurelie's back. "And one for the boys!" another voice crowed.

Aurelie waved at the lutine who'd followed her through the park. They both picked up handfuls of snow and crept around an oak, one on each side, to give snowball earmuffs to an unsuspecting boy. "Girls!" Aurelie called, and ran.

The battle raged through the park, attracting lutins and farfadets and other children who'd heard their friends taking sides. Two black dogs joined in, their wagging tails knocking snow on boys, girls, and Fae alike. Nobody seemed to mind, and when Aurelie emerged from the trees, flushed and laughing, Elise only shook her head.

"I suppose we'll be paying the sausage vendor again tomorrow. The chestnut man and the soup lady brought their carts as well."

"They did?" Aurelie traded her flute case for a towel and dried her hair, smiling behind the white linen.

"As if you hadn't invited them yourself, Your Highness," Elise said tartly. "By the next storm, you'll have all the food carts in the city lined up outside the park to feed the Heir's snowball warriors."

"If I'm hungry, the children must be, too," Aurelie said. Not to speak of Loic, who could eat his weight in sausages. She sniffed. "How about some roasted chestnuts, Elise?"

"Banquet," her maid reminded her.

"You're right," Aurelie sighed. "Another time." She took her flute case and saluted the park, which still echoed with shouts and laughter. This was how a city should sound, she thought, walking toward the palace. With Netta's help, and Loic's, and Garin's, Lumielle would thrive. Aurelie turned her face to the sky, tasting snow and spices and the smoke from roasting chestnuts. It was the flavor, she thought, of happiness.